MW01287369

Creepy Cake Murder

A BITE-SIZED BAKERY COZY MYSTERY BOOK 3

ROSIE A. POINT

Creepy Cake Murder

A Bite-sized Bakery Cozy Mystery Book 3

Copyright © 2019 by Rosie A. Point.

www.rosiepointbooks.com

All Rights Reserved. This publication or parts thereof may not be reproduced in any form, stored, distributed, or transmitted in any form—electronic, mechanical, photocopy, recording or otherwise—except in the case of brief quotations for review purposes.

This is a work of fiction. Any resemblance to actual persons alive or deceased, places, or events is coincidental.

You're invited!

Hi there, reader!

I'd like to formally invite you to join my awesome community of readers. We love to chat about cozy mysteries, cooking, and pets.

It's super fun because I get to share chapters from yet-to-be-released books, fun recipes, pictures, and do giveaways with the people who enjoy my stories the most.

So whether you're a new reader or you've been enjoying my stories for a while, you can catch up with other like-minded readers, and get lots of cool content by visiting my website at *www.rosiepointbooks.com* and signing up for my mailing list.

Or simply search for me on *www.bookbub.com* and follow me there.

I look forward to getting to know you better.

Let's get into the story!

Yours,
Rosie

One

"PUT THE KILLER COOKIE IN THE BAG AND HAND over the cash," I said, nudging Bee in the ribs. Or I tried to. Bee wore a fluffy yellow-and-black-striped bee costume that bulged outward—too much puff for me to reach her side. Her arms poked out of the side-holes of the costume, short and stubby thanks to the extra padding.

I'd nearly died of laughter this morning when she'd come down for breakfast.

"Very funny," Bee said, as she fed another of our Halloween-themed cookies into a bag. She offered the customer who had bought it a smile. "Happy Halloween. Please take a pamphlet."

"What are they about?" The woman asked and lifted one off the countertop. She was dressed plainly, not in costume for Halloween.

"There are stalls set up in the center of town today," Bee said.

"For Halloween," I added in, helpfully. "They're doing an entire weekend-long celebration in Carmel Springs. Dressing up isn't required, but it's heavily favored."

The woman thanked us and walked off, studying the flyer and chomping down on her Halloween-themed cookie. We'd done frosted cupcakes with jack-o'-lantern decorations, skeleton cookies, and even bat candies that turned the customers' teeth red.

It was the 31st of October, and the time had come for spooks and scares and bubbly cauldrons. Business in Carmel Springs, Maine, had never been better. Halloween was the time for candy, toothaches, and tricks, and we were flush with customers.

It helped that we had such a fantastic spot to park the Bite-sized Bakery food truck. We were right on the beach, with the view of the steely gray ocean waves washing over the sand and jagged rocks toward the pier's side.

A cool ocean breeze brushed through the truck, spreading the scent of freshly baked cookies and cupcakes to the surrounding area. We'd gathered two long lines of customers itching to get their hands on our food, and that attention hadn't waned throughout the morning and well into the afternoon.

The next customer in line stepped up, and Millie, the

editor of the local newspaper, grinned at us. She'd come dressed as a witch with a tall black hat and a fake wart glued to the end of her nose. "What do you think?" she asked, turning in a circle.

"You make for an impressive witch," Bee said.

"Don't cast a spell on the truck, unless it's one that will clean up after us," I put in.

Millie laughed. "Unfortunately, I left my spell book at home. I'll tell you what I do need a spell for—convincing the mayor not to let the stalls run until midnight. Most of us have been out in the town center since five this morning."

"You have to stay until midnight?" I asked, adjusting my deerstalker hat. "In this weather?" It was far too chilly to stay out after eight, or maybe that was just me. I'd never been good with cold weather.

"Yes," Millie grumbled. "And most of us have parties to attend. I mean, Franklin's having a big blowout, and everyone's invited. Though, how he and his wife can afford it is beyond me. The holidays are so expensive."

"We were invited too," I said.

"I expect that's because he's currying for favor with the Events Committee," Millie said, rolling her eyes. "You know, there's the decorating competition every year, and the more exposure one gets, the better," Millie paused.

"Say, what are you this year, Ruby? It's obvious that Bee is... well, a bee."

"Very perceptive of you, Millie dear," Bee said, sweet as honey, as she served another customer a cupcake in a pink-and-green striped box.

"I'm Sherlock Holmes." I turned in a circle, tugging on the lapels of my coat. "You were the one who gave me the idea, actually, when you mentioned it last week."

"All you're missing is the pipe."

"Ah!" I withdrew the fake plastic pipe from my pocket and pretended to puff on it. "The guy at the costume shop said I could blow bubbles with this."

"That will be a sight to behold."

I tucked the pipe away again. "What can I get for you today, Millie?"

"I'll have one of those creepy-lookin' cakes. The one with the spider on top," she said.

"Sure thing." I made quick work of placing it in a box for her and handing it over. She paid, made me promise to come by her arts and crafts stall later on, and then hurried off to enjoy her treat.

Two new customers stepped up to the fronts of the lines. One wore a full clown outfit with ruffles around the throat and white makeup that obscured their face entirely, and the other had opted for vampire garb. Fake blood dripped from the corners of the vampire lady's lips, and she wore a sleek black wig, a few strands of blonde peeking out from underneath.

"Good afternoon," I said, merrily, to the vampire. "Happy Halloween."

"Happy Halloween." She smiled, showing off fake fangs.

The clown, who was, quite frankly, straight out of my nightmares, echoed the sentiment to Bee.

"What can I get for you today?" I asked.

"I'd love one of the, hmm, those delicious creepy killer cookies," the vampire said, pointing to the specials board behind me.

"That sounds great," the clown said. "I'll have one too."

I lifted two brown paper bags and turned to the cookie dispenser. A single creepy killer cookie, complete with a candy-coated mask, sat beneath the glass.

"Oh," I said. "I'm sorry. There's only one left. How's the next batch coming along, Bee?"

"It will be ready in thirty minutes."

"I can't wait that long," the clown said, waspishly.

"And neither can I." The vampire lifted her chin. "Excuse me, but I was the one who ordered first. I should be the one who gets the cookie."

"Is that what you think?" Clown turned on vampire. If I'd known who these women were, it would likely have made the situation less humorous. As it was, it was quite something to witness a fake killer clown bearing down on a blood-streaked vampire with the ocean for a backdrop.

"That's what I just said, isn't it?" the vampire countered. "You'd better back off. That's my cookie." She pointed at the other woman.

"No, that's my cookie. Just because you asked first, Theresa, doesn't mean you get to decide who gets the cookie. That's up to Ruby and Bee."

Bee and I exchanged a glance. "Well," I said, slowly, trying to measure my words. "The other cookies will be ready in a half-hour, and there are other treats available. We've got these creepy cupcakes, see? And then there are pumpkin pie slices, as well, with clotted cream."

"That's my cookie." The clown stomped her foot.

"You're acting like a petulant child," the vampire replied, reaching underneath her wig and scratching frantically. Theresa was well-liked but a stickler for the rules. She was barely recognizable beneath all the makeup. "You don't deserve anything sweet when you've got such a sour attitude."

"Please, ladies, calm down." Some of the other customers had started shifting and peering around at the back of the line. The last thing we needed was a fight to drive people away. We'd only just started drawing customers in again after the horrible first three weeks we'd had in town.

"Calm down? Well, I won't be calm until I get what I deserve," vampire Theresa hissed.

"Oh, you'll get what's coming to you, all right." The clown wore a horrible grin, made worse by her red clown lips.

"That's enough." Bee removed the cookie and placed it in the bag. "There's no need to fight. This line is first come, first serve. You'll just have to select something else to eat." She handed the bag, printed with our Bite-sized Bakery logo, over to the vampire.

The clown huffed and puffed and slipped out of line. She stormed off, her bright red hair wobbling in the wind.

"Thank you," Theresa said. "I thought she'd never leave. Horrible woman. I hope I never see her again." She paid and left, as well, and we could do nothing but stare after her, shaking our heads.

"Apparently, tensions are high around Halloween."

"It's the sugar," Bee said, as she turned to serve another customer. "It's a miracle no one's gotten hopped up enough to commit a murder."

I flicked Bee with the edge of a dishtowel. "Terrible sense of humor."

"It's served me well so far." She winked.

Two

"THIS IS MY FAVORITE HOLIDAY." SAM, THE owner of the cozy Oceanside Guesthouse, had outdone us all in the costume department. She was dressed as a knight, wearing a cloak and armor and carrying a longsword—plastic, of course. "I can't wait to get to the stalls and see what they have on offer. I heard there's a kissing booth this year."

I pulled a face. That sounded like the strangest Halloween celebration of all and an embarrassing one. I had it on good authority that Detective Martin, the only handsome police officer in Carmel Springs, would be manning it.

"Come on," I said. "Let's get out there before the sun sets and it gets too cold." We'd been invited to Franklin Smith's Halloween party tonight—this evening would be busy and festive, and, as we stepped out onto the front porch of the guesthouse, I couldn't help the excitement brewing in the pit of my belly.

Sam's guesthouse set the scene too. She had jack-o'-lanterns along the railings, candles lighting their mean grins from within, as well as bats and skeletons and a ghost that flew across the porch with the click of a button.

"Good heavens," Bee said, wiggling her striped fluffy bee butt. "If you don't win the Halloween competition for the best-decorated house this year, it's a crime."

Sam blushed. "I've been trying to win it for three years now, ever since I revamped the guesthouse. I hope this is the year."

"Definitely," I said, looping an arm through hers.

Since we'd arrived in town, we'd had our ups and downs, but Sam had always been there for us, even if it meant dealing with grumpy Detective Jones or murders or break-ins in the middle of the night.

I couldn't wait to move past the drama and enjoy an evening together, as well as the rest of our time in the small town. It was only a few weeks before we'd be moving on to the next place. We still hadn't decided where that would be yet.

Fifteen minutes of walking later, we approached the town's center where the festivities had well and truly begun. Stalls of every kind were manned by folks the Events Committee had hand-selected.

Music thumped from speakers, and children and adults in Halloween costumes roamed around, many of them messing up their makeup as they chomped down on treats or candies. The rich scents of food drifted on the air —everything from cakes and sweets to pumpkin pie and coffee, turkey sandwiches and corn on the cob, butter dripping and melting down its sides.

"I'm glad I didn't get a chance to eat before we came," Bee said, over the music, her hazel eyes alight with excitement.

We strolled past the Haunted House that had been set up in the town hall, spooky writing on a sign declaring that it would be the scariest experience Maine had ever offered. Screams rang out, and I froze then shook my head at myself. The last time I'd been in there, it had resulted in a murder investigation. The chills had passed a while ago, but my kneejerk reaction to screams was envisioning someone in trouble. And police lights. Eek.

You've got to relax, Ruby. Everything's fine.

It was better than fine. It was positively merry.

I joined the line at one of the food stalls, my stomach grumbling for a few slices of roast turkey and gravy. Bee stepped in behind me, and Sam hurried off to go chat with one of her friends at another stall.

"Would you look at that?" Bee poked me in the back.

"What?"

"We're next to the kissing booth stall."

And, indeed, we were. Poor Detective Martin was positioned behind a bat-and-glitter-strewn counter, wearing a knight in shining armor costume, the front grate of his helmet pulled up, revealing his sweat-streaked face. He bent forward and kissed an elderly woman on the cheek. She cooed and patted him on the top of his head, the metal helmet clanging loudly.

"Eugh," I said. "That can't be fun. I wonder how he got roped into doing it."

We reached the front of the line and found Millie in charge, doling out hot pots of turkey and gravy with roasted potatoes on the side, plastic forks sticking from the food. "Hello," she said, grinning broadly. "I'm glad you're here."

"You're working this stall too?"

"Most of them," Millie said. "I'm sort of dabbling. It's great research for articles, and I've got to check that my writers are getting all the details. Last year, we reported that the Taco Stall had served guacamole, and Mrs. Black forced us to do a retraction. Apparently, there hadn't been any guacamole. It was green cream cheese."

"That's..."

"Disgusting?" Millie asked. "It seems that way.

Anyway, the cream cheese was only green from food coloring, but it still caused an uproar. Everyone wanted to know why they hadn't gotten any guac. Mrs. Black became a pariah in the community."

"Over guacamole?" Bee asked.

"People are serious about their food here, dear." Millie paused, brushing off her apron. She nodded to her right. "Did you see the kissing booth?"

My cheeks colored, though there was no good reason for it. "That poor detective."

"Oh, yes, he was talked into it." Millie pursed her lips as she dished turkey into one of the Styrofoam bowls. "Well, 'talked' is a phrase I use lightly. Forced, more like. The yearly Halloween kissing booth is cursed. The person who did it the year before never does it again."

"Cursed," Bee scoffed.

"Why?" I asked. "I mean, why do they never do the job twice?"

"Because they have to wear that horrible getup," Millie said, gesturing to the silvery costume. "And they hardly ever wash it. The struggle is finding someone who fits the suit and who doesn't mind kissing the entire population of females in Carmel Springs, most of whom have saved up all their flirting energy for this tonight."

"Heavens," Bee said. "Shall we join the line too?"

"Of course not!" It took me a minute to register that

Bee had been joking. Once again, I was a victim of her wicked sense of humor. "I mean, no thank you. I came for turkey, not... that."

"One order of turkey and gravy coming up," Millie chimed in. "Minus the kissing."

"Because kissing and turkey do go hand-in-hand." Bee wriggled her eyebrows at me.

I opened my mouth, a scathing response on the tip of my tongue.

A yell cut across the merriment and my thoughts. "Stop right there! You! Stop him. Someone, help!"

I spun toward the noise.

A ripple ran through the crowd of festivalgoers, and a young man, his hair dark and hanging in his eyes, pushed people out of the way, a skeleton with wobbling paper legs tucked under his arm. His lips were painted black, and they parted around a broad smile.

"What on earth?"

But the young man was gone as fast as he'd come, sprinting off into the crowd. A portly guy appeared behind him, huffing and puffing. "Someone! Anyone. You!" He pointed at Detective Martin, who was caught in the clutches of another gray-haired femme fatale. "Detective! Go after that young man, right now. He stole my skeleton."

Detective Martin mumbled something, but the woman who had a grip on his head wouldn't let go.

"Useless!" yelled the ruddy-cheeked man and rushed off.

"What on earth was that about?" I asked.

Millie shook her head. "Looks like that new boy is causing trouble again." She handed over my pot of sliced roast turkey. "Shawn Clark," she said. "He came to town a few days ago, and he's been nothing but trouble ever since. Vandalizing things. Stealing. And did you see that makeup he was wearing? That's not a Halloween costume. Poor Mayor Jacobsen."

"That short guy was the mayor?" I asked.

"The very same. It looks like he's having a terrible Halloween. Serves him right, if you ask me. We're all exhausted. None of us wanted to be here all day," Millie whispered, as she accepted my money. "You two have fun. Try not to get into any trouble."

"No promises," Bee said, as she tucked into a roast potato.

Three

FRANKLIN SMITH'S HOUSE STOOD OUT LIKE A sore skeletal thumb. Now, that usually would have been an insult from me, but since it was Halloween, it meant quite the opposite. The man, who had worked at the local post office for years, had gone all out. His house was covered in spooky lights that glimmered and cast their eerie glow on the identical brick-faced houses on either side of his.

"Goodness," Sam said, as we approached, all still full from all the delicious treats at the Halloween fair. "Look at this place. And I thought I had decorated the guesthouse nicely. Looks like I stand no chance at winning the competition this year, after all."

"Nonsense," Bee said. "The guesthouse looks way spookier than this."

But, privately, I had to agree with Sam's sentiment. I

wasn't well-acquainted with Franklin—he had probably been to the truck once or twice in the past week—but he'd never struck me as the decorating type. He'd been downright mean and closed-off the last time I'd seen him. But I had to give him credit where it was due. The house looked amazing.

And it was even creepier and cooler once we got inside. He'd put out blood-red candles and spooky masks. Jack-o'-lanterns and spider webs hung from the walls and in the corners. The house brimmed with people in their costumes.

The most popular one this year, it seemed, was the clown from *It*, and it gave me the chills. There were so many variations of a mean clown, evil clown, and bloody-mouthed clown that it was hard to keep track of who everyone was.

"Welcome, welcome," Franklin said, appearing in a clown costume as well. He was recognizable only by his bulbous nose and slightly stained teeth. And because he walked through the house with his chest puffed out. "Thank you so much for coming. There's punch in the living room, as well as food on the buffet table. Be sure to mention how much you enjoyed the party to the mayor when he comes by. And how much you love the decorations, of course. Now, if you'll excuse me, I have to go find Emmaline."

"Thanks," I said, but Franklin had already moved off.

"Great host," Bee muttered.

I nudged her in the general area of her ribs, and we wandered into the living room. I grabbed a few cups of nonalcoholic punch and handed them out. It was tempting to stand against the wall, trying to figure out who everyone had come as, but Sam drew loads of attention in her awesome knight costume. Soon, we were surrounded by a gang of clowns and witches and vampires, chatting and admiring her.

"I love this fabric," one of the clowns said, grabbing hold of the thick cloak that hung around Sam's shoulder. The clown's voice was familiar, and I frowned, trying to place it. It was female, light and airy. "Where did you get this?"

"I made it myself," Sam said.

"Well, that's just—"

"Interfering again, are you, Franny?" a second clown asked—this one was large and overbearing, with a belly that stretched the fake blood-stained front of his shirt. "As is your way."

"Excuse me?" The female clown bobbed her head and released Sam's cloak.

Sam immediately stepped back, placing distance between her and the two clowns. A few of the other costumed partygoers gathered around, watching from behind masks or makeup. This was the way of small towns, most specifically of Carmel Springs: People were inquisitive. And they always had time for a fight.

"You heard what I said." The big clown put his fists on his hips.

"Who are you?"

The clown removed his fake nose and glared at her.

"Gregory Michaud," the female clown, Franny, said, tapping her oversized shoe on the carpeting. "What are you doing here? I thought you and your sister didn't attend parties. Too poor, is what I heard."

My eyes widened. *That was mean.* Sam had shrunk back further, and we did the same, watching from afar. The voices of the two clowns were so loud we couldn't get far off enough to avoid being witnesses to the argument.

"You stay away from me, Franny, and you stay away from my sister."

"Oh, please," Franny said, honking her nose. "You just moved to town a few days ago. Don't try to come off as the martyr now. We both know that you only came for one reason and one alone."

"And what's that?" Gregory folded his puffy-sleeved arms. "This ought to be good."

"Money."

A few of the onlookers gasped. One of the vampires took a long, noisy slurp from its punch glass.

"How dare you," Gregory said. "You have no idea... you—you—"

Franny laughed. "What's wrong, Greggie? Cat got your tongue? Seems you're not that smooth when there's no cash to lubricate your lips."

"Good heavens. Who are these people?" Bee asked.

"The big clown," Sam whispered, as the argument continued, "is Gregory Michaud. He lives next door to Franklin, and he's new to town. He moved into his sister's house last week. Theresa. She's such a sweetheart."

"Wait, Theresa? She was the one who was at the truck this morning. She had an argument with a clown over a cookie."

"Who knew that was a sentence you'd say?" Bee took a sip of punch.

"The clown," Sam said, pointing to the smaller of the two, "is Franny Clark. She's Theresa's sworn enemy."

"Sworn enemy?" Bee asked, raising a silver eyebrow. "What is this, a turf war?"

"Well, it would be if Theresa and Franny lived next door to each other. But they don't," Sam continued. "Apparently, the whole argument started years ago, when Franny stole Theresa's husband."

"Whoa. Really?" I asked.

"Yes, though, wait, no... I remember there being something before that. Oh yeah! In high school, Franny pulled a Carrie on Theresa when she was named prom queen."

"Pulled a Carrie?" I asked.

"That means she dumped pig's blood or something all over her," Bee said.

"Oh, disgusting."

Sam put up a finger. "Except it wasn't pig's blood. It was just red paint."

"Good heavens."

A shout rang out from the arguing clowns. "You stay away from my sister!" Gregory poked Franny on the shoulder then spun on his heel and strode off.

Franny rolled her eyes. "Well, that was fun." She gave a sour little laugh then walked off into the crowd, going in the opposite direction to Gregory.

"Goodness," Bee said. "I had no idea people here had time to be sworn enemies."

"Are you kidding?" Sam asked. "Carmel Springs is renowned for its Halloween festival and its sworn enemy duos. There were even famous ones, you know. The Giggler and the Misfit. They came from Carmel Springs."

I tilted my head to one side.

"You haven't heard of them?" Sam asked as the music started up in the living room. Clowns and masked strangers cried out, laughed and clapped their hands, dancing along.

"The Giggler?" I asked.

"Correct. The Giggler and the Misfit. That's what they were known by back in the twenties. There's even a statue of them in the center of town. Basically, they were the first dueling sworn enemies in Carmel Springs. Legend has it, they fought over a lobster fishing boat. The Giggler wanted the boat, and the Misfit stole it from him."

"And then what happened?" I asked.

"They declared themselves enemies and dueled to the death," Sam said, taking a slurp of her punch, "using feathers."

"Huh?"

"Well, they didn't actually die. It was a term they used for effect. The terms of the duel were that the first person to laugh lost the boat. The Giggler laughed first, the Misfit won the boat, and ever since then, Carmel Springs has had a rich history of sworn enemies."

"Wow." What else could I say? I could hardly make sense of it. "So, um, this Franny and Theresa the vampire are carrying on the trend?"

"Correct," Sam said. "Though, I don't think they'll be using the feather duel any time soon. Those two ladies don't go anywhere near each other. Theresa runs the Tea and Cookies Enthusiasts Club and Franny's in charge of the Reading Club."

Before I could ask Sam for more details, a masked matador

swept me onto the dancefloor and twirled me around. I would've been embarrassed, but the spirit of laughter, dance, and fun were thick on the air, and I enjoyed it instead.

After all, it had been such a struggle getting folks in Carmel Springs to accept us. This felt good, even with a pratfall of killer clowns watching my every move.

❧

"WHAT A NIGHT." I LOCKED THE FOOD TRUCK IN front of the guesthouse.

Sam stood in front of it, clutching her cloak around herself in the cold, and Bee made a humming noise under her breath, sounding a little too much like the namesake she was dressed as.

"I need a good cup of coffee before bed," Bee said.

Sam gave her an odd look.

"Bee likes to think that coffee makes her drowsy," I said. "It's one of her tamer quirks."

We trudged up the front steps of the guesthouse, the candles burning low in the lanterns now, and Sam unlocked the front door. There weren't too many people staying at the Oceanside this week, but those who were had their own keys to get in and out.

The hall was warm, and Trouble the kitten meowed

and leaped off the reception desk, his yellow eyes glowing and his tail poker straight. He purred and wound between Samantha's legs then rubbed up against the edge of my Sherlock Holmes coat.

"It's good to be home," Sam said. "We're going to need all the rest we can get."

"What for?" Of course, Bee and I would be out on the beach serving up our creepy cakes, but why would Sam need the rest?

"Halloween in Carmel Springs is an all-weekend event. Tomorrow's Friday. There will be another night of carnival rides and trick-or-treating. And after that, there's the banquet at the town hall. And, oh, of course, I'm having an invitation-only event of my own, as well. There will be plenty of parties too."

"You sure know how to celebrate," I said.

Sam grinned. "We do. But, if you don't mind, ladies, I'm going to take Trouble upstairs. We need our beauty sleep."

"Ditto," Bee said.

But I wasn't tired yet. "I think I'll have a cup of cocoa before bed."

We said good night, and I hurried upstairs to change into my slippers and fix myself a cup of hot cocoa. I came back down and sat out on the back porch, huddling in one of the comfy blankets Sam left out for the guests who liked to admire the view.

There was a lovely one now—the moon hanging over the ocean, the sky cloudless and inky black. Moonlight glimmered along the white sands and highlighted the craggy rocks to the far right. I sipped my cocoa, swilled the warm deliciousness around my mouth, and then swallowed.

Two figures appeared on the beach. They walked along together then stopped then started walking again. One of the figures raised their arms and gestured. The other backed away, folding its arms, from what I could tell. Then they started walking again. The pattern continued until they disappeared from sight, and I frowned. What on earth had that been about?

I shook my head and dismissed it. It was Halloween—the creepiness had gotten to me. Carmel Springs was pretty safe and people walking along the beach together was a normal thing.

Still, the strange question marks remained in my mind until the cocoa was finished, and I was sleepy enough to go up to bed.

Four

BEE AND I HAD OPTED NOT TO WEAR A SECOND set of costumes for the next day of the Halloween celebrations, but it seemed we were the only ones. We'd pulled up on the beach that morning to find ghouls, ghosts, and vampire slayers waiting to buy treats.

Folks took the celebrations seriously in Carmel Springs. But it was kind of nice, if I was honest, to think that there was such a sense of community in the town.

"Happy Halloween," the first customer said, as she accepted her green and pink striped box.

"And to you." I waved and dusted off my apron.

It was still early, and the morning customers who liked to pop in before they hurried off to work were gone. We'd have a reprieve of about fifteen to twenty minutes before the new set of customers arrived.

"Here you go." Bee handed me a hot cup of coffee. "On the house."

"Can I get one of those cupcakes on the house too?" Not exactly the healthiest breakfast around, but it sure was delicious.

"Would you like the spider-topped cupcake or the one with the skeleton? Or a black cat?"

"Black cat will do just fine," I said.

Bee handed one over, and I immediately peeled back the paper and tucked into it, relishing the sugary, buttery goodness of the frosting. Bee had one too, and we ate our cupcakes, sipped our coffees, and studied the shoreline.

It was a cloudy day but glimmers of sunlight broke through every now and again and played across the ocean. This view was a treat, and I could appreciate it now more than ever thanks to the fact that business was finally back on track.

Bee yawned behind her coffee cup. "I'm too tired to function today. All that Halloween excitement was too much for me."

"You'd better get used to it. According to Millie, there are loads of festivities lined up. And did you see the way that vampire slayer looked at me? Clearly, we should have remained in costume for today."

"There's no way I'm dressing up as a bee two days in a row."

"Why not? I thought it was cute."

"And sweaty," Bee said. "And I kept knocking into things and getting stuck in doorways. Besides, the joke's over. It was cute for one day, but for two? That's just gratuitous comedy."

"Heavens, I didn't know you were a joke snob."

"You learn something new every day," Bee chuckled.

She was right about that. I had learned something new about her every day since we'd started working together, probably because I'd known so little about her to start with. Bee's background was still a mystery to me, and I wasn't one to pry.

We finished off our coffees and readied ourselves for the next set of customers.

A flash of something on the ocean caught my attention, and I searched for it. But no, there was nothing there. Just my imagination. For a second, I'd been sure there had been a black thing floating in the water.

Head in the game, Ruby. You've got sales to make and a life to enjoy in Carmel Springs.

The customers arrived in drips and drabs at first, but the crowd of folks seeking out their morning sugar rush soon swelled around the front of the food truck.

Coffees, cupcakes, and treats were served, money was tendered, and people left happy. The ebb and flow of food and customers was interrupted by a shrill screech. And then another. And another.

The cries hadn't come from the gulls now gathering near the benches, but from the people nearest them.

"What's going on?" a man called out.

Another shriek rent the air, and then the crowd parted enough to give me a brief glimpse of the water and the beach.

My heart fluttered.

"Not again," I whispered.

"What is it?" Bee nudged closer, holding a customer's half-filled coffee cup. Not that it mattered. Just about everyone had turned from the truck to stare at the beach.

"It's a body," I said. "Another dead body."

And indeed, on the pale sand lay the corpse of... a vampire.

Five

"Everyone stay back. Stay back! This is officially a crime scene." Detective Jones stood where the overlook petered off into the long sandy trail that led to the beach.

The police had already set up a line to cordon off the area, and the body had been shielded from view. Naturally, the crowd of onlookers around the food truck had doubled—news traveled fast in Carmel Springs.

Another murder. And on the beach right in front of our truck.

"He can't pin it on us this time," Bee said, placing a hand on my back. "Don't worry, Rubes."

"I know, but still." I gave her a look, my face cold likely because I'd gone pale. "Another murder. Here. And we witnessed it again."

"We didn't technically witness it." Bee sighed and walked to the coffee pots. She poured steamy, life-giving liquid into two cups and brought them over. "Look on the bright side. At least this time they weren't killed with your marzipan."

I shuddered at the thought—in the short while we'd been in town, we'd had our fair share of brushes with murder. "I wonder who it is. How terrible."

"Really unfortunate, isn't it?"

"I feel bad for the people in this town. They can't catch a break."

Bee snorted. "It's got me thinking ... just what kind of murder town did we come to?"

I pinched Bee's elbow. "Things happen. It's not like the town is inherently evil."

"Hmm. Maybe it's cursed."

"Maybe you've been reading too many spooky stories." I'd caught her asleep in an armchair in her suite, a spooky horror book propped open on her chest.

"It's Halloween," Bee whispered. "I'm allowed to enjoy a little pulse-pounding fiction."

"Except you've got dark circles under your eyes," I said. "Oh, don't look at me like that. I'm just worried about you. You're my star baker and my friend. I hate seeing you tired and cranky."

Bee's frown broke, and she offered me her signature

gap-toothed grin instead. "Fine. You wore me down. I'll cut back on the scary stories, but that doesn't change things."

"What do you mean?"

Bee nodded to Detective Jones who stood with his fists on his hips, talking to one of the bystanders—one of our customers who held a Bite-sized Bakery Box in trembling fingers.

"I get the feeling that Jones is going to find a way to pin this on us," Bee said.

"Impossible. This time, we weren't anywhere near the body." I paused, rolling the cardboard coffee cup holder against my palms. "I can't stop wondering who it is. The victim, I mean."

"I might have an answer for you." Gray-haired Millie, the editor of the local paper, appeared. She'd opted for a butterfly costume today, complete with multicolored wings that wobbled as she moved. One of them struck a customer, who yelped and side-stepped as if Millie was about to pounce. "Sorry, dear. Ooh, everyone's so jumpy."

"I can't imagine why," Bee said.

"You have a smart mouth, dear, and thankfully, a smart brain to go with it," Millie replied. "You mentioned the death? What did you see?"

I broke it down for her—there hadn't been much time

to witness anything. There was the scream, the body, and the cloak.

"A Halloween costume," Millie said.

"Assuming, of course, it's not a real vampire we're dealing with here."

"Bee, I told you, you're reading too many of those spooky stories."

Millie leaned one arm on the countertop, her wing bobbling behind her. "Now, there were several vampires roaming around last night, but I have it on good information that one of them went missing in the early hours of the morning."

"Oh?" My eyebrows arched.

"Theresa Michaud," Millie whispered. "I was up late last night, helping the Cleaning Committee sort out the stalls after yesterday's debauchery, as well as managing the ambulance calls."

"Ambulance calls?" I asked.

"Oh, Detective Martin passed out from heatstroke," she replied, waving a hand like it wasn't of any consequence. "But while I was there, I heard one of the wives of the on-duty police officers complaining that she had to clean up by herself. Apparently, he was meant to come help her out but couldn't because a missing person's case had just been filed for Theresa Michaud."

"I thought you had to wait a day or something before

you reported someone missing. We saw Theresa yesterday morning."

"Oh no," Millie said, waving again, "that's just what Hollywood wants you to think. You can report someone missing right away, especially if they went missing under suspicious circumstances. So, I think we'll find that the body of the vampire is, in fact, the body of Ms. Michaud."

"Wait a second," Bee said. "That's the same Theresa who Sam told us was in the midst of a non-range war with the clown from last night, Franny. They had a fight over the cookie yesterday morning, right?"

"That's my best guess." Already, the cogs whirred in my mind.

Theresa, the vampire, had been fighting with Franny, the clown. It was easier to categorize them as costumes in my mind since I wasn't exactly best friends with either of the women. Bottom line was they had been sworn enemies according to the local gossip mill, and who better as a prime suspect but the sworn enemy of the victim?

And last night, there had been an argument between Franny and one of Theresa's relations, her brother.

"Uh oh," Bee said, as she poured another cup of coffee and handed it over to Millie. "Looks like Ruby's getting in the zone."

"Thinking of following the trail?" Millie asked. "Heaven knows, the more you hinder Jones, the happier we all are. The minute he solves a case, he becomes insufferable. Wants to run for the office of Police Chief. Mayor Jacobsen is at his wit's end with the man."

"I don't know," I said. "It's not my place."

"Well, if you change your mind, I might know a little something extra regarding Theresa's untimely demise." Millie's bright blue eyes shifted. She scanned the waiting crowds, checking for eavesdroppers. "Apparently, Franny's nephew was arrested this morning. Not sure what for, but it's a little suspicious, don't you think, that he would be arrested right after his aunt's sworn enemy is found washed up on the beach? Shawn Clark," Millie continued. "You saw him last night, remember? At the stalls? The mayor was chasing him."

"Hmm." Bee tapped her chin.

Jones had finished interviewing the folks closest to the beach and marched off now, casting one last furious glance at the truck. He disappeared into the blue crime scene tent that shielded the body from view.

I fell into silence, my gaze stuck on the tent.

Just who had killed Theresa Michaud? Surely, one cookie wasn't enough to spark a homicide? It was none of our business anyway.

"For once," I said, "we're not actively involved in a case. I say we stay out of it. It's better this way."

Bee let out a disappointed huff. "If that's what you *really* want."

"Well," Millie put in, "if you ladies *are* thinking of looking into it, you know where to get your information." She turned to leave but paused, looking back over her multicolored, glittery wing. "And just so you know, I mean, if you dears are curious, Theresa Michaud's house is right next door to Franklin's, just off Main Street. You can't miss it."

And then she was gone, and I was left with an itch to find out more that I shouldn't.

Six

AT NOON, BEE AND I CALLED IT A DAY ON THE truck. Nobody was buying any treats or coffees, as most were too nauseated by the sight of the forensic tent to even consider eating. A sign of a healthy mind, in my opinion. Who could eat at a time like this?

Theresa was dead, and we'd had a front-row seat.

"This is amazing," Bee said, chomping down on a powder donut and sprinkling confectioner's sugar all over her lap and the passenger seat.

"How can you eat right now?" I asked. "And how is it you're so messy while you're eating?"

"I'm nervous-eating. It's the third body that's shown up in Carmel Springs in the last month and a half. Do you mind if a woman sates her nerves and fears with a few donuts?"

Donuts, I had established, were Bee's favorite treat. That and hot cocoa with mini-marshmallows. "You know, you'd swear you were a cop."

Bee froze, mid-chew, sugar coating her lips. She coughed and a little puff of white dust erupted from her lips. "Why do you say that?"

"The donuts?"

"Oh. Oh right," she replied and gave an awkward laugh. "I'll clean it, by the way." She gestured to the mess on the passenger seat.

"I know you will." I smiled at my friend. She was strange and fun to be around. Wasn't that the best combination one could find in life? Someone who kept the interesting conversation alive but was trustworthy and loyal.

I parked the food truck in front of the Oceanside Guesthouse, anticipating a long bath to ease the knots of tension from my shoulders. Whenever Detective Jones was around, my insides hurt a little. I'd half-expected him to come charging over and question us. Or to accuse me of being involved and close down the truck. He'd done that once before.

"Yum," Bee said, finishing the last of her donut. She got out of the truck and proceeded to dust off her seat.

I exited too, taking a deep breath of the fresh ocean air. It soothed me, and the nerves and nausea had abated somewhat—I had never been good with all things icky. That had been one of the reasons I'd left my job as an investigative journalist. I'd seen far too many dark and depraved events. Now was the time for sweets and candies, comfort and success.

A banging came from the front of the guesthouse.

Sam stood on the porch, desperately tugging at the end of a roll of orange and black crepe streamers that had gotten caught in the door.

"—no, no, no," she said, under her breath. "No. No!"

"Sam?" I hurried over. "What's going on?"

The owner of the guesthouse gave another great tug, and the crepe paper tore in half. She stumbled and nearly fell backward but steadied herself on the railing. "No," she said, meeting my gaze, her dark hair in disarray.

Samantha was big on first appearances. She kept her guesthouse and herself neat at all times, and she wasn't flighty either.

"What's going on?" I walked to the door, opened it, and removed the rolls of crepe, bringing them out to her. "You know, you could have just fetched—"

"I know that." She snatched them from me. Her bottom lip quivered, and her anger dissolved. "Oh, Ruby, I'm sorry, I didn't mean to snap. I'm just so frustrated."

"Why? What's going on?" Bee had finally finished dusting the donut sugar out of the truck. She came up the steps, frowning. "Wait a second, this isn't right." She peered around. "What happened to your jack-o'-lanterns?"

My eyes widened. I'd been so concerned about Sam, I hadn't even noticed that most of her decorations were just... gone. "And the spooky ghost! The skeleton. The mummy? Where are they?"

"I don't know," Sam wailed. "And that's why I'm so upset. I woke up this morning and they were just gone, and it's a disaster. A total disaster. I'm supposed to have everyone over tomorrow for my Halloween party and banquet. I invited the mayor, for heaven's sake, and the head of the Events Committee. One look at this place, and they'll rule me out of the competition for good."

"Don't say that," I said. "We'll help you fix this."

"Yeah!" Bee put up a sugar-dust tipped finger. "We'll go to the General Store and get more decorations."

"That's sweet, guys, but it's no use. There's no way Old Man Lester's place will have anything I can use. I have to face facts. It's over. Over before it even began." Sam hung her head, dropping the rolls of black and orange streamers to the porch.

Trouble danced out of one of the windows, leaped, and attacked the rolling paper.

"Don't say that, Sam," I said. "Come on. We're going to find a way to make this better. We'll fix it. Right, Bee?"

"Right. We'll go out there and see if we can get you some new decorations. You go make yourself a cup of tea and have a cookie. We'll be back before you know it."

"Are you sure?" Sam asked, the first glimmer of hope appearing in her gaze.

"Positive," I said.

And with that, Bee and I set off into town, walking the long road toward the General Store on Main Street, clutching our coats to ourselves. It was better to walk—I'd had too cupcakes this morning and about five cups of coffee with half-and-half. Working off the calories was a must.

"Poor Sam." I tucked my hands into the pockets of my puffy pink coat. The wind tugged at my shoulder-length hair, brushing it back from my ears.

"I wonder who did it."

"What? The murder?"

"No," Bee said. "The decorations. Someone had to have stolen them. They can't have just vanished into thin air. Perhaps it's one of the other folks in town who wants to win the competition?"

We turned the corner, and my heart skipped a beat, cutting off what I'd been about to say. Franklin's house was up ahead, and that meant that Theresa's place would be next to it. I nudged Bee, gesturing toward Franklin's done up Halloween home. "Remember what Millie said?"

Bee's eyes lit up. "Hmm. But which house is it?"

We had slowed significantly—anyone who peeked out of the houses on the suburban street, flanked as it was by the sidewalk, wrought iron lamps, and trees shedding their golden-brown leaves, would think us strange. Or suspicious.

On one side of Franklin's house sat another that was done up in Halloween style, with a pumpkin-head knocker of all things. And on the other...

An old house that looked as if it had seen better days. A smashed pumpkin lay on its side in a yard that was all dry grass. The windows bore drawn curtains, the door needed a swipe of polish, and the porch stairs looked like the kind that would creak.

A battered mailbox had been perched on the crumbling brick wall. "Michaud" was printed across it in bold letters.

"Well," Bee whispered. "I guess we have our answer."

"What happened? It looks like it hasn't been lived in for months. Or years."

"Smashed pumpkin, though. And look at the mailbox. See how it's on its side with the wooden pole still sticking out of its end? Splintered too. Looks like someone vandalized the place," Bee said.

A door slammed further down the street and spurred

us into action. We hurried off, me occasionally glancing back at Theresa's house.

If it had been vandalized, then who had done it? And why?

Seven

THE INSIDE OF THE GENERAL STORE WAS NEATLY decorated, the only hints of spider webs were the fake ones Old Man Lester had put up in the corners in celebration of Halloween. The aisles were stocked with all the necessities and even a few imported and specialty items I wouldn't have expected to find in a small town like Carmel Springs.

It was a sign of a business owner who cared for himself, his business, and the people of the town, and I admired that.

"All right," Bee said. "Now, let's see if there's anything we can find."

We grabbed a shopping cart from the front of the store and pushed it down the aisles, me pushing, Bee walking and stopping as we searched the shelves for Halloween décor. We entered the aisle containing stationery and found the last vestiges of decorations there.

A single plastic jack-o'-lantern, more orange and black crepe, and a set of creepy, blood-red candles.

"Oh wow," I said. "Sam wasn't kidding. There's nothing here. What are we going to do?"

"It's not looking good."

"We can't give up. We promised Sam we'd come back with something." I paced to the section that held the stationery, frowning. Cards, pens, scissors, glue, glitter. There were all sorts of things we could use to make home-made decorations. But would that be enough?

"What are you thinking?" Bee asked.

"Two things," I said, putting up my fingers. "That we create something with these supplies and pumpkins, if Old Man Lester still has some in stock, and that we bake creepy cookies and varnish them."

"Varnish them?"

"You know, cover them in polish so that they don't spoil. We can bake all sorts of crazy things and hang them up around the place."

"Oh!" Bee exclaimed, lifting a finger. "We could turn Sam's Guesthouse into a real-life witch's house. You know, from that old fairytale, Hansel and Gretel? That Brothers Grimm story."

"It's a big task, but, if we focus, we might be able to get

the whole place ready. We have the rest of the afternoon and the whole of tomorrow until the evening," I said, excitement bubbling in my stomach.

This would be a great way to take our minds off the whole "murder" thing. And to make Sam happy. Apparently, there was a cash prize for the winner of the Halloween Day Competition. Likely, Sam wanted to use that to revamp the guesthouse and make the place even better.

She'd been such a lovely host, supporter, and friend that I was more than happy to help her out.

We hurried into the fruit and veg aisle. But it was empty of pumpkins—that was to be expected on Halloween.

"What now?" Bee asked, shifting the items around in our cart.

"These," I said, lifting a melon and tapping against its thick shell. "They'll be difficult to carve, but if we're careful, we can make a few lanterns and paint them orange. They'll look sort of spooky and cute."

"You're a natural at this." Bee grinned at me, and we started loading melons into our cart, stacking them carefully so they wouldn't disturb our other items.

"OK, so I think we—"

The intercom blared and crackled overhead, and a stern voice sounded throughout the store. A woman who'd been sniffing the cantaloupes and knocking them with her knuckles let out a squeal and dropped one.

"Attention shoppers," the voice said. "Attention all shoppers. This is Lester, and I am interrupting your shopping experience to let you know that there has been a murder in Carmel Springs. Theresa Michaud has been killed. You have been warned."

The cantaloupe lady let out another cry. She dropped her handbasket and skedaddled out of the fruits section back toward the front of the store. The door clapped shut a second later, the bell tinkling.

"Good heavens," Bee said. "What an announcement to make."

"I heard Old Man Lester did that type of thing." I paused, holding a melon in both hands and squeezing gently. "I wonder ... do you think he might know something?"

"About what? Decorations?"

"No. What happened to Theresa. Maybe he knows something we don't. The store is sort of hub. A lot of information probably comes through these doors."

"Good idea," Bee said, her eyebrows rising. She was animated, likely at the thought of something as exciting as investigating another murder. What was it with her and that? She seemed so experienced too—during the last investigation, she had taken photos of the crime scene and made deductions I wouldn't have.

I placed the last melon in the cart, and we hurried to the front of the store.

Old Man Lester stood behind the counter, frowning at the cash register.

"Hello," I said, trying to be cheerful. "We heard your announcement."

Old Man Lester shifted, his gray eyebrows crinkling over deep brown eyes. "You're them bakers. From the truck."

"That's right."

"You helped solve that murder of the lobsterman," he said.

"Correct again," I said. "It's nice to meet you."

"You too." He sniffed, staring at us. "You going to pay for that stuff?"

"Sure are." I helped Bee unload our goods onto the counter, and Lester did the relevant calculations using an old calculator. He tapped the amount into his register, and I paid, my pulse racing. What if he didn't want to talk to us about what had happened? He didn't seem friendly.

"Do you know anything about what happened to Theresa?" Bee was impatient at the best of times—she didn't beat around the bush when it came to asking questions.

Old Man Lester froze, his hand extended and holding my change. "No. But I got something that might interest you two ladies."

"Oh?" Bee and I exchanged a glance. "What is it?"

"I'm thinking that you two might want more information 'cause you're interested in figuring out who offed her. Am I right?"

I pressed my lips together. "Not technically. We were just curious."

"Follow me." Old Man Lester shuffled out from behind the counter and marched down one of the aisles until he reached a door. We followed him into an office that had little to no ventilation and a single chair and desk. An open laptop sat atop it.

Lester beckoned for us to gather around. "See here? This is where I view my surveillance footage from the store. And if I go back two days ago..." He clicked and tapped away on the keys, his gnarled fingers spry. "Watch this."

Gray surveillance footage opened on the screen. "That's Theresa, see? The one with the gray-blonde hair?" He tapped on the screen, and white bloomed underneath his fingertip. "And watch, here she comes."

Another woman entered. She wore her hair dark and

short but was relatively tall herself. She stopped the minute she spotted Theresa standing in front of the counter.

"Who's that?" It was difficult to identify anyone out of costume, especially if I hadn't met them before.

"That's Francesca Clark," Lester said, pressing his finger to the screen again. "Watch 'em fight."

"Fight?" The word had barely left my mouth when chaos erupted on the screen.

Franny launched herself at the blonde, short Theresa. The fight was insane, women clawing at each other, their faces masks of anger. Finally, Old Man Lester appeared onscreen and managed to separate them. Franny fled. Theresa remained, her hair standing up at odd angles.

"There you have it," Lester said. "Now, some might not think that's evidence, but I sure do. If anyone wanted to see Theresa dead, it was Franny."

"Did they usually fight like this?"

"Nope. First time I seen it," Lester said. "You mark my words, it was that Franny. She hated Theresa's guts, and everybody knew it." He sniffed. "I'm only surprised the cops ain't arrested her yet."

Eight

"THEY'LL BE HERE ANY SECOND!" SAM SQUEAKED, her makeup starting to run. Tonight, Sam had chosen to be not a knight but a witch, and her tall, pointy hat was skew atop her head. Her dark hair was curled, and she'd pasted a wart on the end of her nose. "Oh my gosh, oh my gosh."

"It's OK, Sam," I said. "The place looks great."

And it did, if I did say so myself. Bee and I had spent the whole of yesterday baking treats to be polished and hung around the guesthouse. Sam had cored out the melons, painted them, and created interesting decorations. The Oceanside had been transformed into an evil witch's gingerbread house.

The guests were due any minute—a selection of the local townsfolk, the committee members, and guests, including the mayor himself. And Sam had created a menu that would surely impress.

"I have to get back into the kitchen. Look after Trouble, will you? Make sure he doesn't do anything crazy?"

"We're on it," I said, sweeping the calico kitten into my arms. I stroked his head, and he purred, bumping it into the palm of my hand. I was back in my Sherlock Holmes costume, and Bee was done up as a bee with a big, fluffy yellow-and-black butt.

How she expected to sit in one of the chairs and eat was a mystery to me, but the fact was, we had done it. The place looked amazing. We'd even painted some of the light-bulbs in hues of red and orange to create a spooky ambiance, and Millie had sacrificed some of her candles to help solidify the witchy effect.

A half an hour passed, and the delicious scents of cooking drifted through the guesthouse. A few of the new guests, a couple named the Carlingtons, and a young woman, Kayla Thatcher, drifted down wearing their costumes and talking among themselves.

The guesthouse's front doors were open, and I hovered near the curtains in the living-room-cum-dining-room. Cars pulled up and parked either side of the food truck, and the guests started emerging. Franklin Smith appeared, tall and slightly overweight, his chest as puffed out as it'd been at his Halloween party, wearing the same clown costume as he had then.

Mayor Jacobsen, who was short and round and moved like a boat rocking on the water, shuffled out of a fancy black SUV. He wore a chef's outfit, strangely, which didn't seem like much of a costume to me.

The guests entered, and music tinkled from a stereo in the corner. There were nameplates at each table, and Bee and I found ours.

We were seated with Franklin, the man who'd hosted the Halloween party the night before, and Gregory, who was out of costume, his forehead wrinkled and his eyes bloodshot. Of course, the poor man had lost his sister yesterday. He shouldn't have been here.

Then why is he?

The kitchen doors opened, and Sam gave a shy welcome to everyone, bobbing her head and blushing almost magenta. Afterward, a group of servers, most of whom had come from the Chowder Hut, emerged carrying the starters.

I licked my lips. It had been a hard two days of work to set up the amazing Halloween décor around the guesthouse, and I was ready for my reward.

A waiter placed a bowl brimming with delicious seafood chowder in front of me, and I had to restrain myself from tucking in right away.

"What's this?" Franklin said, leaning in and sniffing his bowl.

Bee pursed her lips. She wasn't good with anyone who offended her friends, however slight that offense might be. "It's a delicious chowder," she said, "and knowing Sam, it will be the best we've ever tasted."

"I second that," I said.

Gregory lifted his spoon, dipped it into his chowder, and lifted it to his mouth, almost mechanically. He chewed, swallowed, and repeated.

"Are you all right?" I asked.

Immediately, Gregory dropped his spoon with a clatter. He glared at me then scraped his chair, got up, and marched off.

"That was tactful," Franklin said. "You could have waited until he'd finished his meal."

"Hey," Bee snapped, "that's not her fault. She was trying to be nice. Anyway, he shouldn't be here if he's not in the state to attend."

Franklin slurped chowder off his spoon noisily. "I suppose you're right, but I doubt that he's *that* emotionally distraught that he couldn't attend this... event."

I didn't like the way Franklin said it, nor the way in which his eyes roved over the interior of the guesthouse. He didn't seem impressed by anything.

"Why do you say that?" I asked.

"Oh, come on, you must have heard the rumors," he said. "No?" He ate another spoonful of chowder and chewed on a piece of crusty, buttered bread. "Everyone in town wants to know who would do it. You know, hurt Theresa. After all, Theresa was well-liked in Carmel Springs. Of course, not as well-liked as she should have been. Franny hated her for sure. So did a few others because Theresa was ... how do I put this? Kind of a stickler for rules. And a neat freak."

I kept my face impassive. If Theresa had been such a neat freak, why had her house been such a mess? Was that a clue in itself?

"What's any of that got to do with Gregory?" Bee asked, impatiently.

I nudged her under the table. If she pushed too hard, Franklin might get suspicious, and who knew who he was friends with. What if it was Jones? What if Jones heard we'd decided to check this out?

Shoot, is that what we're doing?

"Gregory's relatively new to town. He only moved in a week ago." Franklin paused, chowder dripping from his spoon, suspended above his bowl. "I'm not much for gossiping, but I did see something interesting on the day he arrived."

"What did you see?" I was too intrigued to care whether this was gossip or not. How was I supposed to figure out what had happened to Theresa without asking difficult questions?

"Theresa lives next door to me, you know, and she's usually so quiet. Like I said, sticks to the rules, keeps her yarn and home neat. She usually decorates too, but this year, she sort of let things go—and that coincided with her brother's arrival." He set down his spoon and wiped his fingers off on the tablecloth. "When he got here, he had a huge fight with Theresa right in the front yard. He wanted to put—" But Franklin broke off.

Gregory had returned, his eyes dry and his bald spot gleaming by the candlelight. He took his seat and started eating again, ignoring the rest of us completely.

Franklin pursed his lips and returned to his chowder. I averted my eyes to keep from staring at Theresa's long-lost brother. He had been having fights with her. Or, at least, one fight. But then, siblings fought all the time—we would have to establish an actual motive for him wanting to harm his sister.

Gregory dabbed under his eyes with his napkin. He sniffed and left half of his chowder in the bowl.

Was he grieving?

Or does he have something to hide?

Nine

So far, our suspect list was relatively short.

There was Gregory Michaud, Theresa's long-lost brother—but we had little evidence to back up the claim that he might have murdered her. He'd been emotional and had a fight with her once. That was all we had.

And then, of course, there was Franny Clark, who had definitely gotten into an altercation with Theresa in the General Store and in front of our truck.

Given that it was a Sunday, and just about everyone was done with Halloween and had retired to their homes, it felt to me like the right time to investigate. We didn't have any treats to sell on the truck today, and I'd given up on pretending that I wasn't interested in the mystery.

Bee and I strolled down the street, affecting a casual

attitude, even as we approached the perp's house. Bee called Franny the "perp," even though we didn't have any solid evidence that she'd committed the crime.

Yet.

The wind brushed against my coat, and I tucked it tight against my body as we approached Franny Clark's home. The real shock had come this morning when I'd asked Sam for Franny's address and discovered she lived right next door to Franklin on the other side. Her home was the one with the pumpkin-shaped knocker.

How bizarre.

Or was it serendipitous?

"Are you ready, Rubes?" Bee asked, as we trudged up the front steps and halted on a welcome mat with swirling writing.

My stomach did a swirl of its own, but I forced the nerves back. "Let's do it."

Bee lifted the knocker and brought it down three times.

Nothing happened. No footsteps or calls from within.

I pressed a finger to the doorbell and it chimed inside the house.

"Just a second," a woman called out. "One second." And then a whisper, "You shouldn't have come here today. This is ridiculous. You know how bad this makes me look, Shawn."

My eyes widened. Shawn? The very same Shawn who had been arrested the night before Theresa's murder? That was what Millie had said. And he was here. Of course, they were family. Did they live together?

The door cracked open and Franny Clark appeared, her dark hair tied back, her eyes hawkish and the tip of her nose sharp. Then again, that had been hidden underneath a clown's nose the other night. "Yes?"

"Hi," I said. "We wanted to come offer our condolences for losing, um... Theresa. Your neighbor." It was a weak excuse, and even I knew that.

Franny raised a penciled eyebrow. "Excuse me?"

"We're here to offer our condolences," I repeated.

"No you're not," she replied, nasally. "You can't be. Everyone in Carmel Springs knows that Theresa and I hated each other. Which means that you're here for another reason." She lifted a finger and jabbed it in my direction. "To interfere! To get the next scoop of gossip to spread among your friends."

"We're not from here," Bee said.

"Yeah, sure. I saw you two on that food truck. You wouldn't give me a cookie. And if you think I'm going to talk to you about—"

A dark figure materialized behind her, and I gasped—a man in a cloak and hood and... no, it was just that same dark-haired, dark-eyed teenager we'd seen at the Halloween

Festival. His hair hung in front of his face, and his lips were colored dark black. He pushed past Franny and then past me.

"Excuse me," Bee said.

"You're excused." Shawn marched off down the stepping stone path and out onto the sidewalk, the gate clattering closed behind him. He reminded me of a giant bird of prey—the same skulking walk. Predatory, almost.

"How rude." Bee pulled her coat straight. "How absolutely rude."

Franny's ire seemed to have faded, or rather, been redirected. "Yeah, I'm sorry about that," she said. "He *is* rude. My sister's child who came to stay with me. He can't get a job, anywhere. Not that he's trying very hard, but the point is, he's been nothing but a nuisance to me since he arrived. Apparently, he got in trouble over in Boston, and he had to leave."

"What type of trouble?" I asked.

"I don't know, and I don't ask," Franny said. "Honestly, he's not even living with me. He's got an apartment somewhere in town. He comes to visit once a week to check in, just so that when his mother calls, he can say he's been visiting me. Not that I want him to." She shook her head. "Back when I was nineteen, I was motivated and hard-working. Shawn is a good-for-nothing nobody. He doesn't help out around my house, he doesn't work, he doesn't pay bills. I don't know how he's survived for so long."

It was a diatribe I hadn't been prepared for, but it was still information.

Shawn was clearly poor. Did that mean he'd have wanted to kill Theresa for money? Perhaps frame his aunt for the murder, since there was no love lost there?

But did Theresa even have money to steal? Had her house been broken into before her death? There were too many missing elements here.

"Anyway," Franny said and clicked her tongue against her teeth. "Is there anything else you wanted? Other than to spread useless rumors about me?"

"No," Bee said.

"We didn't want to spread rumors about you."

"I'll believe that when... well, never. I'll believe that never. Now, good day to you, and get off my property." She slapped the door shut in our faces.

Bee and I stood in silence for a moment.

"Do you think she's still mad because we didn't give her the last cookie the other day?" I asked.

Bee sniffed. "Frankly, my dear, I don't give a flying raccoon."

"I suppose you're right," I said. "Come on, let's go back to the guesthouse and have some coffee and treats."

We set off down the stone, taking the same path that Shawn had.

Shawn who had definitely stolen a decoration from the festival, the other day. Who had been arrested, supposedly, after Theresa's murder. Did Jones know something we didn't?

Ten

WE MADE IT TWO STEPS DOWN THE SIDEWALK, away from Franny's house and past Franklin's, when the noises started. A crash and a bang, and then someone yelling out in pain. Bee and I froze mid-stride, and her hand clamped down on my arm.

"Someone's in trouble."

The noises had come from Theresa's house. The front door crashed open, and a cat streaked from the interior of the house carrying a mouse in its mouth. It darted around the side and out of sight.

"You get out of here you cat freak!" Gregory Michaud jogged down the front steps, the thatch of hair surrounding his bald spot glistening with sweat. He wore a sleeveless vest, the middle stained with sweat and a pair of jean shorts that had gone out of fashion in the year 2000. Gregory's pasty hands were bald into fists.

I relaxed, slowly, and Bee let go of my arm.

Gregory said a word I didn't care to repeat, even mentally, and spun toward the house. He caught sight of us and stumbled. His foot struck the rotting pumpkin lying in the middle of the path, and he fell forward with an unholy shriek.

Gregory slapped into the ground, and the pumpkin gave an unattractive squelch of protest, spilling its seed guts all over his legs and bare feet.

"Good heavens," I whispered.

Bee pressed a hand over her mouth to keep from laughing.

"Are you all right?" I called, jogging forward. I entered the yard—if it could be called that—and helped Gregory from the ground.

He grumbled and shook off his legs. "Stupid thing. Stupid..." He took a breath. "It's that cat. It keeps breaking into the house and running amok. What am I supposed to do about that?"

"Maybe you should try getting rid of the rats." Bee leaned on the crumbling stone fence, one eye narrowed. "If not for the cat break-ins, for health and safety."

Gregory folded his arms. "Who are you?"

"We met the other day, at, um, Sam's Halloween

dinner. I'm Ruby, and this is Bee." I stuck out a hand and regretted it.

Gregory's palms were stained orange from where he'd scraped the rotten pumpkin from his legs. Thankfully, he passed on the handshake. "Right. What are you doing around here?"

"We were just chatting with Franny," I said. "Giving her our condolences."

"What for? From what Theresa told me, Franny hated her."

"You two spoke often?" I asked.

"Well, yeah. She was my sister." He cleared his throat. "And she was having loads of trouble with her neighbors. That Franny wanted to start a range war, but Theresa avoided it." He paused, eyes narrowing. "I don't know why I'm telling you this."

"It's just idle chatter," I said. "But we do want to offer our condolences to you too. Theresa used to come by the food truck and grab treats."

"Oh right! She told me about your cupcakes and cookies," Gregory said, his demeanor altering, right away. "She loved them. Told me they were the best cookies she'd ever tasted."

Bee cleared her throat. "Well, that's very kind of her."

A sad silence followed. Poor Theresa.

But just because Gregory's being nice doesn't mean he's innocent.

"You should come by to the truck this week," I said. "We'll be opening again soon, you know, after the holiday, and we'll give you a few cookies and cupcakes on the house. Won't we, Bee?"

"Sure thing. Flattery will get you everywhere."

"Thank you," Gregory said, and he seemed genuinely grateful. "I'm not great at cooking, and money's been tight around here ever since Theresa passed. You know, she was the one with the job."

"I'm sorry to hear that. You know, if you're in need of work, you should check the listings board at the General Store."

"Thanks, but I'm fine. I'm just waiting to hear from the executor of her will. Theresa left her assets to me." He ran his fingers over his bald spot. "I hate that Theresa's gone, but she did right by me when she put me in her will. Obviously, nothing will replace what she meant to me as a sister."

"It sounds like you had a great relationship. Good for you," I said, leading him as gently as I could.

"Oh, I guess you could say that. Sure. Theresa and I had only recently reconciled, about a year ago, and she'd been telling me to come stay with her for ages. She was alone, you know, and I think that was difficult for her. That's why she got that stupid cat."

I struggled to keep a straight face. First the will and now this: he didn't want to look after his dead sister's cat? Horrible.

"Oh, it's fine," Gregory said, waving a hand at me. "I put food out for it and everything, but it's going to be an outdoor cat now. That's all. Finally."

"Wasn't it before?"

"No." A muscle in Gregory's jaw twitched. "That's the only thing Theresa and I consistently disagreed on. That cat is a plague. It used to watch me. And it used my bed as a toilet."

"Goodness."

"Exactly." Gregory offered me a quick smile. "Anyway, nice talking to you. Thanks for coming by. I'll definitely come out to your truck sometime soon for those cakes!" He gave a final wave and marched off back into the house. The door clapped closed.

"That was... interesting," Bee said.

"Is that what we're calling it now?" I joined her back on the sidewalk. "I'd have called it suspicious."

"Written into his sister's will, strange change in aesthetic at the house according to neighbors, the cat didn't like Gregory." Bee ticked off on her fingers. "Animals usually have a great sense for people, you know."

"Oh, I know." The kitten at the guesthouse, Trouble, had helped me take down a murderer, just by his reaction to the man in question.

"And he doesn't like cats. That's another serial killer trait if I ever saw one."

"Jeffrey Dahmer liked cats."

"How, in the name of all that is donut, do you know that?" Bee asked.

"It's Halloween. I thought you liked being creeped out." I laughed at her expression. "I saw it in a documentary once. Oh, all right, I'm sorry for bringing him up. Back to donuts. And the cat-hater in question."

"Never trust a cat-hater," Bee grumbled.

I peered up at the front house, noting how all the curtains were drawn, shut for what? To avoid people looking in?

Gregory was definitely a person of interest now. He had argued with Theresa, he had only just moved in, and he'd seemed fine today as opposed to when he'd come for dinner at Sam's. What did that mean? Had something or someone at the guesthouse upset him? Or was there another secret he had to keep?

"You're staring off into space, Rubes."

"Right. Sorry. I'm considering the options. Let's get back to the Oceanside." The morning was still young, and there would be plenty of time to contemplate Gregory's connection to his sister's murder. If there was one in the first place.

We headed off down the street, taking a detour down Main Street for the sake of it, occasionally waving at people we recognized from the truck. Some of them stopped us to ask when we'd be opening up again, and it filled me with warmth, knowing that we mattered to the townsfolk now.

They cared about us. And I cared about them.

Discovering who had murdered Theresa was more important than ever.

Eleven

The Oceanside Guesthouse looked just as fabulous in the morning light as it had the night before. It was the last day of the awesome Halloween celebrations. Folks had dressed up in their costumes and walked down to the pier for the grand reopening of the Lobster Shack.

I definitely wouldn't be going to the restaurant anytime soon—my last experience with the place hadn't been great, especially since it had involved a killer. And if the same man still ran the restaurant, that would mean no lobster rolls for the foreseeable future.

Together, Bee and I entered the guesthouse to the welcoming scent of fresh-brewed coffee and baking cookies. Chocolate chip, by my nose.

"Smells like we're in time for brunch!" I rubbed my

palms together, both to warm them after the fall chill and to prepare for the deliciousness that would surely follow.

Trouble padded out of the living room and meowed at me. He wound between my legs, purring and rubbing against me in greeting. I loved this little "hello" from him. He seemed to have taken a liking to me.

That was lovely, because I'd always wanted a cat, but my ex, Daniel, would never have allowed it. Now I couldn't stay in one town long enough to have a pet—or rather to let a cat own me. Having Trouble around was still lovely.

We entered the living room and waved to the Carlingtons in the corner where they sat sipping from mugs and nibbling on muffins.

Sam appeared in the kitchen doorway bearing a smile. "Good morning," she sang. "Would you like some chocolate chip muffins?"

"And two coffees, if it's not too much trouble," Bee said.

"Sure!"

Sam returned with our muffins and coffees a second later—I'd been wrong about the cookies, but the muffins were just as good, with gooey chocolate pieces inside, still warm from the oven. Sam left us to eat, while Trouble curled in front of the fire.

Bee snagged a newspaper from a table over and set to

reading while she ate, picking at the muffin with her fingertips. "Of course," she said, "they're already making grand deductions about who it might be and what actually happened. Listen to this ... strangulation before drowning."

"Eugh." I pushed my plate away. "That's off-putting."

"Yes, it is. But it does give us more information."

"How so?"

"Don't you think it's interesting that Franny had that fight with Theresa in the General Store? That looked pretty intense. Physical. And clearly, whoever killed Theresa had no problem getting physical."

There were suspects galore again. Could it be that Theresa's long-lost brother had had something to do with it? Gregory now had an official motive, to my mind, but why would he have done it in that particular way? He was an obvious suspect. Would he risk murdering his sister so soon after he had moved into her home? And what was with the lack of Halloween decorations and the sudden dilapidation?

And then there was Franny, who definitely appeared to have a motive: rage. And what about Shawn Clark? Could there have been a reason for him to have done it?

"I wonder if Theresa was rich," I said, sipping my coffee. "After all, if she was, there might have been a motivation. Could someone have robbed her? Perhaps things got out of hand?"

"Hmm. Her house looked broken-down, but, on the flip side, Gregory seemed happy at the prospect of getting money from the will. I don't know, actually," Bee replied, turning the page, "but I do know that strangulation is quite personal. I mean, it's not like a gunshot or something."

"I guess." I pulled a face.

"Hmm."

"What?"

"Nothing, just that, apparently, there's an award ceremony tomorrow. For the Halloween Day Competition! Oh, that's exciting for Sam. I hope she wins." Bee looked around the living room, smiling. "We'll have to go."

"Yes, we will." I finished off the last of my coffee.

Halloween was on its way out. No doubt the Christmas decorations would be up in the stores within minutes. I could almost hear the Michael Bublé songs. It was strange to me that the stores seemed to forget all about Thanksgiving and move right on to Christmas.

I chewed on my bottom lip, peering around at the decorations. "I wonder if there's any other evidence we can find," I said. "There must be something we can discover. Maybe we should talk to Millie again."

Bee nodded. "We're not going to have much more time to think about this anyway."

"What do you mean?"

"Well, we'll be leaving town soon. Unless..." Bee leaned in, pressing her empty muffin plate aside.

"What?" I asked.

"Do you want to stay in Maine for Christmas? Or would you prefer to go back to New York to see family and the like?"

"Wow," I murmured. "I hadn't even thought of that. Honestly, I don't have any family to go back to at the moment. My mom and I haven't spoken years. But what about you? Don't you have someone you want to see over the holiday season?"

Bee shook her silver-haired head. "Not a one. I haven't had the best track record at making friends."

"Until now," I replied, smiling.

"Until now," Bee agreed.

Trouble meowed and darted into the dining area. He took a leap onto my lap and settled in it, purring and massaging with his furry paws.

The Carlingtons got up from their table and headed out with the intent of taking a walk down to the pier, and Bee stifled a yawn behind her coffee cup. We'd had a late night last night, celebrating the Halloween festivities.

"I think I should stretch my legs," I said. "It will give

me time to mull things over. Do you want to come along for a walk, Bee?"

"No, thank you. I think I'll curl up in an armchair by the fire and read, um, the paper."

"Bee, I'd better not catch you with another of those scary stories. You know they've been tiring you out."

"You won't catch me," she replied with a wink.

I laughed, rose from the table, and thanked Sam in the kitchen for the delicious brunch. I gave Trouble one last scratch on the head then started out for my walk.

Hopefully, the sea-kissed air would wake me up and give me some fresh ideas about the case.

Twelve

I STROLLED ALONG THE ROAD, AWAY FROM THE guesthouse and toward the Chowder Hut. It would be closed on a Sunday, but it wasn't like I planned on visiting and chomping down on a couple of their famously crunchy breadsticks. Though, that would be nice.

Shoot, I'd just had a muffin, and I was already hungry again.

Come on, Ruby, think. Whodunit?

I broke down the suspect list in my mind again, but no answers were forthcoming. Whether I liked it or not, I didn't have any other leads or evidence. The only hint that anything had been wrong was that Shawn Clark guy, the dark-haired and makeup-wearing young man who'd stolen the décor at Halloween.

But stealing and murder were two different crimes and not necessarily linked.

Oof, maybe I'm in too deep. Good heavens, I don't need to solve this crime. It's not threatening the truck or anything.

I'd grown attached to some of the people in Carmel Springs. Now that the suspicion had been lifted from our shoulders, people in town had warmed to us. Millie was so sweet, and Sam was a treasure, and almost all the guests had been wonderful so far. Even Mayor Jacobsen was kind and jovial—he'd talked loudly about how delicious the food was at the guesthouse and how fantastic the decorations were.

The thought of folks in town being afraid because of the murder upset me. And it didn't sit right that there were secrets lurking in this cozy town. It was my background—a terrible habit to get into, solving mysteries and uncovering the truth.

Hadn't I quit my job to avoid exactly that?

The thoughts and my feet carried me along the winding road toward the rocky outlook where the Chowder Hut sat. Next to it, there was a lookout point that would give me a view of the ocean.

I drew level with the restaurant, and a flicker of motion caught my eye.

I paused. *What was that?*

The Chowder Hut was definitely closed. There were no cars parked out front, and the windows were dark.

A sharp tinkle of glass breaking came next, and I froze, my palms growing sweaty.

Someone was breaking into the restaurant. It had to be...

I crept toward the source of the noise, pulling my cellphone from my pocket. I unlocked the screen, my finger hovering over the touchscreen. I could easily call Detective Jones. I had his number, thanks to the previous run-ins we'd had with him.

But a break-in didn't necessarily equal anything related to the murder. So why call him? It would be better just to call 911 and report the incident. The dispatcher would send out regular cops, and I wouldn't have to see Jones at all.

Shoot, it might not have been a break-in at all. It might have been a bird crashing into the sliding glass doors.

There was only one way to find out.

I walked around the side of the restaurant, past the wooden walls that rattled in the wind, and the windows that looked in on the friendly interior, complete with buoys hanging from the walls.

Another shuffle of noise reached my ears, and this time, I did hit the button to summon the cops.

I rounded the corner and spotted the bottom half of a human being—legs ensconced in blackened jeans—sticking out a window. They kicked and struggled. The intruder had gotten caught on the sill.

"Hey!" I cried, dropping my phone and running forward. For once, I wasn't frozen in fear—perhaps it was the thought of the burglar getting hurt on the glass that had driven me into it. By the time the idiocy of my actions registered in my mind, it was already too late.

My hands hooked around the guy's legs, and I brought him backward. Using the moves I'd learned in my karate training, I incapacitated the guy, leveraging his weight against him. And it was a man. A young man. I caught his hands behind his back and held them there, pressing him into the ground on his stomach.

He struggled and cried out through the balaclava covering his face. "Let me go!" he whined. "Let me go."

"No." I couldn't reach my phone, but the screen was still lit up. My call had connected. I shouted out my address and the situation, not daring to release my captive in case he somehow got the better of me. This was ridiculous. What had gotten into me?

I'd never been one to run toward danger.

Too late to go back now. But who is it? Who's the criminal?

I ripped the balaclava from the man's head.

Shawn Clark glared up at me, the dark kohl around his eyes stark against his pale skin.

"I SUPPOSE YOU THINK THIS WAS CLEVER?" JONES snarled, his hands on his hips. He was at least a head shorter than me, and I was by no means a tall woman. "I told you, Holmes, I told you not to interfere with my investigations."

I blinked.

Shawn had already been taken away in a police cruiser, and it was just my luck that it was Jones who had turned up to the crime scene with his partner Martin.

"I wasn't interfering in anything," I said. "I was just walking by and I happened to see him here."

"And you expect me to believe that? I know you were following him."

"I most definitely was not. Why would I be?"

Jones's already thin lips drew into an even thinner line. "I wasn't born yesterday, Holmes. I know what your kind is like."

"What's that supposed to mean?" Likely, he meant people who had come for the tourist season in Maine.

Once, he'd called me a leaf peeper. "I swear, this was just a coincidence." But it was mightily intriguing that Jones thought I was interfering because Shawn was involved. Did that mean that Shawn was an official person of interest in Theresa's murder? "Look, Detective Jones, I have no interest interfering. Why would I? I—"

"That's enough." Jones drew his hand through the air in a slicing motion. "I've been waiting for something like this to happen, and I was right to think it'd go down."

"Go down?" Bee would've had a sarcastic comment to counter that statement, but I was fresh out. My palms were sweat-streaked. I'd just apprehended a criminal and made a seriously poor judgment to handle it myself. What if he'd had a knife? Or a gun? What if he'd overpowered me?

"You're coming with me," Jones said, crunching forward across the grit at the back of the restaurant. He took hold of my arm. "I've had enough of you."

"What? No." I drew my arm from his. "If you need a statement from me, just take it here. I don't have to go down to the station."

"Oh yeah, you do," Jones said, a cold glint in his beady eyes.

"What? Why?"

"Because you're under arrest for interfering in an ongoing police investigation." Jones flashed a smile. "I warned you, Holmes, but you wouldn't listen. Now you're going to pay the price for your gossipy, interfering ways."

I had no choice but to go with him, that or risk having another charge smacked on top of the first—resisting arrest. My mouth had gone dry and, heavens, my brain had too.

Thirteen

MUCH TO DETECTIVE JONES'S ETERNAL ANGER and my equaling relief, he didn't have any right to hold me for longer than twenty-four hours. There simply wasn't enough evidence to hold me for longer than that, or even to charge me with interfering with an ongoing investigation.

"I'm sorry about this," Detective Martin said, under his breath, as he escorted me down the front steps of the police station, away from the holding cell that had been my bedroom for the night.

An incredibly uncomfortable and horrible-smelling bedroom. I had never missed Bee, Trouble, Sam, or the guesthouse more. What had I been thinking, going after the intruder? In a way, Jones had been right, as much as I hated to admit it—I should never have been involved.

"Really, Miss Holmes, you have my sincerest apology for my partner's behavior," Martin said. "I know this must be frustrating for you."

"He was within his rights to hold me on suspicion of being involved," I replied, bitterly. And I was never bitter. Unless it was about my disappearing ex-fiancé, Daniel.

Martin opened the passenger-side door of his cruiser for me. "Please, allow me to give you a ride back to the guesthouse."

I hesitated. "I'm fine walking." Though, the last time I'd gone walking, I'd wound up intercepting a burglary. *But what was Shawn trying to steal in the Chowder Hut? Surely, the safe would've been emptied for the weekend.*

"I insist," Detective Martin said. "It will make me feel a whole lot better about how you were treated."

I sighed and thanked him, slipping into the passenger seat. It was a vast improvement on sitting in the back behind the horrible grate that separated the two sections.

Martin got into the car and started the engine. He pulled out onto the street and drove past folks shopping or sipping coffees in the Corner Café. I resisted the urge to sink down in my seat—it wouldn't matter either way. Knowing Carmel Springs, everyone and their granny's uncle's brother knew that I'd been arrested yesterday.

Hopefully they hadn't gotten confused as to why. *What if they think I killed Theresa?*

"Jones was apoplectic with rage when he realized he had to let you go," the handsome detective said, breaking the silence.

"Oh." I licked my lips. "He shouldn't have arrested me in the first place. I was trying to be a good citizen."

"I think Jones is trying to be one too, in his own way."

I didn't care to agree with that sentiment. He'd been nothing but mean since we'd met him, but he was likely an OK cop. Apart from the whole "arresting me out of frustration" thing. "I don't understand why he thought I was interfering. Was it because of Shawn?"

Detective Martin glanced at me askance. "I'm not at liberty to say much, but Shawn is definitely a person of interest. In several crimes."

Now, that did intrigue me. At least I'd learned something of use during this experience. "I assume thievery is high on the list of crimes?"

"Can't say."

Instead of rolling my eyes at him, I looked out of the window at the activity near the town hall. Of course! Today was the announcement of the winner of the Halloween Day Competition. Sam would be excited about that—I was thankful that I'd make it back in time to go with her.

The cruiser pulled up outside the Oceanside. We'd barely parked before the front door slammed open and Bee stormed out, wearing her fluffy bee costume, her gaze on fire with the fury of a thousand droplets of boiling fudge taste-tested before they were cool. *There's nothing quite as painful as a sugar burn.*

"You'd better go," I said. "She'll flay you instead of Jones. You've got a uniform, so it won't make much difference to her." I got out of the car, and Detective Martin screeched off.

"Let me at 'em!" Bee growled, but the car was already gone. Detective Martin knew what was good for him. Bee stamped her foot and almost looked ready to chase after him. She grunted after a second. "Come here." She drew me into a brief hug. "Are you all—ooh! Poo!"

"Poo?"

"You smell terrible." She stepped back, holding her nose. "You'd better go upstairs and shower before the award ceremony. You can tell me all about Jones's crimes on the way there. It will help me decide on a fitting punishment for him."

"It's nice to see you too, Bee," I said, managing a laugh.

Suspicion brewed, simmering unanswered. I was close to something. I could almost sense it. It had to do with money and with Shawn. With Theresa too. Gregory? Maybe.

But what was the answer?

Fourteen

FOLKS HAD GATHERED AROUND THE STAGE THAT had been erected outside of the town hall. Everyone wore their Halloween costumes in celebration of the final announcement. The faces of clowns and goblins and witches and minions were filled with hope and excitement.

Children, who had clearly had far too much sugar, darted through the crowd, laughing and playing. The sound was a lovely and slightly annoying backdrop to the chatter and the odd shout from one of the onlookers for Mayor Jacobsen to "get the show on the road already."

Sam stood in her witch costume, shifting her weight from one foot to the other, and Bee looked about ready to breathe fire. "The nerve of that man," she muttered, every now and again. "He had better not be here today. He had better not be here." She broke off and sneezed violently.

"Are you OK?" I asked. "Are you coming down with something?"

"Rage." Bee sneezed again. "That or I'm allergic to Detective Jones."

"Really, Bee, you can't let him get to you like this."

"I can and I will. He needs a reality check. He can't even keep control of his own cases," she said.

I'd already told her about Shawn Clark's strange break-in at the Chowder Hut and Detective Martin's hint that he might have somehow been connected to the murder. It seemed open and closed to me, but I wasn't a law enforcement expert.

Who else could it be?

I scanned the crowds, searching for familiar faces, and spotted Franklin Smith and a squat woman with styled cherry-red hair chatting off to one side. The owner of the Chowder Hut, a tall, thin woman who wore a Joker costume, was to our left. Detective Martin was positioned near the front where Mayor Jacobsen had taken to the stage.

Many of the other faces were familiar—people I had served on the truck, or who had become brief friends or acquaintances in passing. It was a nice feeling, standing among them, but I reminded myself not to get too comfortable.

I'd taken it upon myself to tackle Shawn to the ground

when, really, it hadn't been my place. Was it because I'd become too attached to Carmel Springs and its people?

The mayor tapped on the microphone, and it squealed.

"Good heavens!" Bee cried and sneezed for the third time.

She was definitely coming down with something.

"Attention everyone," Mayor Jacobsen said, clearing his throat repeatedly. "I'd like to welcome you all to the final event in our Halloween Day celebration."

A smattering of applause rang out. "Get to it already!" someone yelled. "Who won?"

"All right, all right," Jacobsen said, flapping a slip of paper from the breast pocket of his matrix-style trench coat. It was quite something to see a man of his size dressed as Neo from the hit movie trilogy. "I've got the results right here. The winner of the Halloween Day Competition is decided by the vote of the Events Committee."

People shifted. Samantha let out a little squeak and crossed her fingers, nearly dropping her prop broom in the process.

"This year's decision was reached by a unanimous vote. Or the results were unanimous. Either way, there was a clear winner."

I peered around and spotted Franny Clark standing a short way off, wearing no costume at all. Shawn was behind her, apparently having been bailed out, his arms folded, and a nasty cut streaking along the back of his right hand. He scowled at me.

"Come on," Sam said. "Please, please, please, let it be me. Please let it be me."

"It is my great pleasure to reveal, with no further ado, that the winner of the Halloween Day Competition for 2019 is none other than..." He opened the envelope and extracted a slip of paper.

The tension was so thick it could've been cut with a knife. Even I held my breath.

"Samantha Pringle!"

Sam's jaw dropped.

Shouts of joy and applause thundered around us. Bee and I shrieked and clapped our hands. We drew Sam into a hug and helped walk her up to the front. She ascended the stage's steps, visibly shaking, and posed for pictures with the mayor and the committee members, holding a massive check.

"This is amazing," I yelled.

"Justice at last," Bee said, over the shouts and laughter. "Poor Sam needed a pick-me-up after the trouble in town over the last few weeks."

Sam's cheeks were pleasantly pink, and she smiled from ear-to-ear, blinking back happy tears. It was so good to see a friend happy that I welled up as well. I wiped the tears from under my eyes, laughed, and clapped. Bee beamed. The Carlingtons were nearby too, and Mr. Carlington lifted two fingers to his lips and whistled shrilly, his wife giggling at the noise.

Most of the townsfolk cheered along as the photographers snapped photos, but some of the attendees didn't look that happy. Millie was one of them, interestingly, and so was Franny, though I could hardly tell if that was just her state of being or not. Shawn was gone.

None of that mattered, now. We'd done our part to help a friend in need. This called for a celebration—hot cocoa, creepy cakes, and an hour of warming ourselves by the fire. The murder investigation could wait. So could the mystery of what Shawn had been doing in the Chowder Hut.

Couldn't it?

Fifteen

"THANK YOU SO MUCH FOR YOUR PATRON-achoo!" Bee sneezed and scattered coins over the food truck's front counter. She gasped for breath and scrambled a Kleenex out of the pocket of her apron, dabbing the end of her nose. "Sorry about tha-choo!"

"Thachoo?" the customer, a young woman, backed away from the change. "Listen, you keep it. I think I'm going to, um, yeah. Go." And she hurried off, leaving both her change and her neatly packaged cupcake behind.

"You forgot your foo-choo!" Bee sneezed again, blocking it with her tissue. She turned away and erupted into a volley of sneezes, one after the other, and the few customers we'd gathered early this morning backed away.

"Looks like that's all she wrote for our breakfast-cake-eaters," I said. "Bee, I told you not to get out of bed this morning."

"You can't manage the truck by yourself," Bee said, sounding as if she'd spoken through the end of a horn. "I can't let you-choo!"

"You very well can let me choo," I said, pretending to be a train conductor and honking the horn.

"Bery funny."

"Bery nasal," I replied. "Look, we need to get you to a doctor. One or two days off the truck isn't going to make a difference. Halloween was fantastic for business, and your health comes first."

Bee sneezed a fiftieth time and grimaced, reaching for a fresh Kleenex.

"That and the health of our customers. I'm going to have to quarantine the truck and scrub it down after this."

"I'm fine," Bee said, watery-eyed.

"That's enough stubbornness out of you. We're going. Now get in the front before you contaminate anything important."

Bee mumbled under her breath but bustled out of the side of the truck. The passenger-side door slammed a second later.

I cleaned up the counter, shut the window of the truck, then made my way to the front too. We took a slow drive through town, past the Cleaning Committee members and volunteers getting rid of the last of the streamers and stalls, and toward the doctor's practice near the small cove at the opposite end of town.

We parked outside the squat, white-walled building, and I guided Bee out of the truck and into the reception area. The office was the same as any other I'd been in, with magazines, chairs that were likely saturated with enough germs to infect a small village, and a water cooler that had been well-used.

But the reception desk was empty.

"You go sit over there, Bee."

For once, my baking partner didn't argue. She tottered over and sat down, dabbing at her nose and eyes, sneezing, and generally feeling sorry for herself.

I leaned over the edge of the reception desk. "Hello? Is anyone here? I have a sick friend who needs some help."

"One moment please!" a frantic male voice called out. "Ouch, oof." A clatter of noise came from the door behind the reception area. It opened, and a blond man with an exceptional polka-dotted ascot came out. "Hi there," he said, tossing his hair back. "Sorry. There's usually two receptionists out here to man the desk, but since Emmaline went and got herself fired..."

"Emmaline? What is that, a drain cleaner?" Bee called.

"She's rude when she's sick," I said, by way of apology. "Emmaline's a lovely name."

"Well, Emmaline wasn't a lovely person, so what does that matter?" The receptionist didn't have on a nametag, but his attitude told me all I needed to know about him. He didn't like his job, and the easier I made this, the better.

But something strange had sounded in my mind. A bell had rung. Emmaline. That was a unique name. Who did it belong to? I'd heard it somewhere this weekend. But where?

"Emmaline," I said.

"No, I'm Warwick." The receptionist pointed at his chest. "Warwick." He drew the name out slowly.

"But who's Emmaline?" I asked.

"Drain cleaner," Bee chirped. "Now, can I please have an appointment? I'm only dying of typhoid fever over here."

"Don't be abrasive, Bee," I said.

"Like drain cleaner?"

I rolled my eyes. "Sorry, um, Warwick, do you have any availability for her to see a doctor? We're kind of desperate."

"Oh sure," Warwick said and sat down in his chair, tapping on the screen. "Let me see what I can do for you."

"Faster, please." Bee sneezed.

"I can squeeze you in to see the doctor in like ... fifteen minutes?" Warwick sighed. "Sorry, things have been tough ever since Emmaline got fired."

"Fired," I said.

"Yeah, she was so crazy. Like... so erratic. And I caught her stealing from the vending machine. Can you believe that?" Warwick flicked his hair back again. "Totally out of control. When the doctor found out she'd been doctoring the books as well, that was it for her. But she was fired like, last week, and it was such short notice that we haven't found anyone to replace her yet."

Bee let out a terrific sneeze, one so destructive that Warwick actually jolted on the spot.

"Sorry," I said. "You OK, Bee?"

She gave me a deathly stare.

"Right. So, you were saying?" I asked.

"Nothing. Just that we need a new receptionist. You wouldn't happen to be interested, would you?"

"Sorry, no."

Warwick shrugged. "Worth a shot. You can wait over there for the doctor, by the way. He'll be with you shortly."

"Thanks," I said and strode over to join Bee. I sat down next to her, balancing my chin in my palm. There was just something about that name. Who was it? Where had I heard it before?

Emmaline. Who are you?

It was silly. What did the receptionist matter? She had nothing to do with anything.

Sixteen

"Now, you stay curled up right there in front of the fire. You heard what the doctor said, Bee. Lots of rest and fluids."

"Doctor's a hack," Bee insisted. "I'm fine." But she still didn't try getting up from her spot next to the fireplace in the Oceanside Guesthouse. Trouble had opted to curl up right on top of her feet, and Bee had been given a side table on which to place her water and pills. She sneezed and dabbed, sneezed and dabbed. "Really, I'm fit as a fiddle. I'll be on the truck by tomorrow morning. I'm just having allergies is all."

"What did the doctor say was wrong?" Sam asked as she trooped out of the kitchen, carrying a bowl of chicken soup. She'd started making it the minute she'd heard the news that Bee was ill.

That news had come on gossip-wings from the folks who'd nearly gotten infected by flu cakes this morning on the truck. "Just the flu," I said. "She just needs to rest and drink water. I mean, it's normal at this time of year, isn't it? Especially for people with weak immune systems."

"My immune system takes offense to that." Bee's complaint was barely audible.

Sam set down the chicken soup on the side table. "There you go. Eat it all up, Bee. It will help you feel better. Ooh, I'll get you a soda."

I followed Sam into the kitchen, my curiosity drawing me along. I'd been in the kitchen once before, to bake cupcakes for a wedding that had never taken place—due to the fact that the bride had died before it could. The rush of baking back then had blurred out most of the details.

The kitchen was lovely and spacious with granite-topped counters, wooden cupboards, and a spectacular view of the ocean through a back window that was next to the rear exit of the building.

Sam paused at the sink and washed her hands. "Better to be safe than sorry," she said. "Let me get that soda for Bee. It's such a pity she's ill. I know it sounds silly, but I hope the other guests don't catch it."

"Oh, that doesn't sound silly at all." But perhaps my next question would. It would seem out of the blue. "Sam, I wondered if you could help me with something."

"Of course, anything." Sam extracted two sodas from the fridge and smiled at me.

"Right, so I was wondering if you could tell me if you know of anyone named Emmaline? It sounds familiar, but I don't know who that is."

"Oh, sure, that's—"

The bang of someone thundering across the back porch interrupted Sam, and a dark figure rushed past the window.

"What was that?" I asked. "Who was that?"

"I don't know," Sam replied, pale in the face.

"Wait here. I'll check it out." I hurried through to the living room, where Bee had already fallen asleep, and then toward the glass sliding doors that let out onto the back porch. The door was locked tight. I opened it and peered out. My eyes widened.

All the furniture on the back porch had been slashed and hacked apart. The bang had clearly come from the sofa, which had been thrown onto its side. The back of the guesthouse had been trashed.

Sam came out and let out a shocked cry. "No! Why? Who would do this?"

I could only shake my head. I had no idea.

"So, you're telling me that you just happened to be here when this stuff was torn apart?" Detective Jones asked, clicking his ballpoint again and again as if that would change what had happened. Or maybe, he hoped it would magic me away.

No luck there for either of us.

"Yes, that's exactly what I'm telling you," I said, trying to remain calm. It had been a long morning, what with Bee's illness and then the vandalism. None of what had happened made sense to me, but my gut told me that it had to do with the case.

Just what it was, however, I wasn't sure. And mentioning that to Jones would send him into a fit of rage.

The detective stood in the center of the living room, occasionally glancing out at the mess in the back of the guesthouse. Other officers combed over it, but it didn't seem like they'd have a 'solve' any time soon.

"You saw a dark figure," Jones said, without writing it down. "You expect me to believe that."

I pinched the bridge of my nose, offering up a prayer for strength. "I don't expect anything from you, detective." I hadn't meant for it to come out as an insult, but there it was.

Bee, who had either been asleep or feigning it, cracked an eyelid. "Ah. He's back. The rotten apple of my eye. The hobbit straight out of the Shire. The one and only detective with the worst case-solving record in Carmel Springs."

"Don't try my patience," Jones said, pointing at her. "I'll arrest you."

Bee sneezed into a tissue. "You'd have better luck arresting a mountain lion."

Jones grimaced and took a step away from her. "You didn't tell me she was sick."

"Oh, right, I forget that updating you about my friend's health is on the list of conversation priorities between us."

"That's the sarcasm I like to hear," Bee said.

"Look." I put up a hand. "I've given you my statement. There's not much more for me to tell you, detective. I don't know who did it, but whoever they were, they clearly wanted to get back at Sam."

"You leave the deductions to me," Jones growled then stamped off toward the back of the Oceanside.

I lowered myself into an armchair across from Bee, shaking my head.

"You know, I never get tired of seeing that man," Bee croaked. "He's truly the light of my life."

I managed a laugh, but Bee didn't seem to note that it was mirthless. Her eyes had already drooped closed again, leaving me to consider the strange vandalism and the clues, or lack thereof, that I had left to dissect. If only I could figure out how these strange incidences were connected.

Seventeen

THERE WASN'T MUCH FOR ME TO DO WITH BEE being sick and no food to serve on the truck. Sam had already closed up the guesthouse for the afternoon, the police were gone, and the alarm company was on its way out to install a system for Sam.

I tucked my hands into my pockets and opted for a long walk past the pier and along the beach. There were plenty of quaint homes, stores, and even a library that overlooked the ocean—rocks or sand, neither mattered. The view was gorgeous.

The afternoon had come, but the sun, while bright, didn't do much to warm me up. The wind was biting and my ears stung.

What's the answer?

Franny? Shawn? Or Gregory?

Once again, I had no evidence. Ridiculous. I couldn't do anything without actual evidence. Franny had hated Theresa, and Shawn was clearly a troubled young man. Gregory had been in Theresa's will.

I slowed. I had reached the end of the long street, where it circled up and around back into town. The last building on the right was different from the others. The sign on the front was slightly decrepit, but the words were still clear.

The Helping Hands Soup Kitchen.

That was nice. I hadn't known there was an initiative in town like that. Bee and I could help out too. Perhaps we could deliver a few cakes or cookies to the soup kitchen to hand out to the homeless?

I sat down on the bench across from the soup kitchen, trying to gather my thoughts. But it was no use. The questions I'd had earlier had slipped from my grasp.

Emmaline.

Shawn?

Wait a second. Shawn! The young man strolled down the street, the collar of his dark faux leather jacket popped. He stared directly ahead, not breaking focus. He dipped into the soup kitchen.

What was that about?

He's hungry. Maybe that's why he tried to break into the Chowder Hut. And that made me kinda sad. The poor dude had no job, and if he wasn't staying with his aunt, Franny, then where did he live? Heavens, I couldn't be feeling sorry for him now. What if he was the murderer?

The thought prompted me to my feet.

I hesitated for only a second—there was no Bee to run in headfirst here and take the heat for me. I was on my own. I headed across the street and entered the soup kitchen. The melamine tables were mostly empty, apart from one where Shawn sat, bent over a tray that held a slice of bread and a bowl of soup.

He dipped the bread into the bowl, hungrily, and ate, his fingers shaking.

Guilt wracked me. Something wasn't right with this picture. The guy had been arrested twice since he'd come to Carmel Springs, and now, he was in a soup kitchen, starved. And so young too. Where had I been at nineteen? In a better position, for sure, with a good education and a future ahead of me.

I rounded the table and sat down across from Shawn.

The makeup-wearing teen froze. He lowered his spoon slowly, eyes narrowing. "What?"

"Hello," I said.

"What?" he repeated.

"I think we got off to a rough start."

"You tackled me to the ground and called the cops. You're a snitch."

"No, I'm a concerned citizen," I said, slowly. "My name is Ruby Holmes, and I—"

"I don't care what your name is. You're just like the rest of them."

"Like who?"

Shawn brushed his pitch-black hair back from his pale forehead. "The rest of the people in this town. My aunt, that stupid detective, the mayor. Y'all think that I'm some kind of bad guy or murderer, but you don't know me."

Another wave of guilt beset me.

"None of you care what I have to say," he continued, "so why don't you save me some time and leave before you say something that will annoy me."

"You didn't murder Theresa, did you?" It was more of a statement than a question. I hadn't had a chance to speak to Shawn. I hadn't done my due diligence, but then he hadn't exactly been approachable, and Halloween had been so busy.

Shawn glared at me. "Duh. Of course I didn't, but I'm just the easy target, aren't I? That detective wants to believe it's me. It will look real neat if they can pin a murder on me instead of just petty offenses."

That did sound like a distinctly Jones move to make. He wanted everything easy, and while that probably wasn't true for his partner, it still didn't fill me with faith that Jones was any closer to solving the mystery than I was.

"You know," Shawn said, dipping his spoon into his soup and lifting it to his lips, "if you give me some money, I'll tell you what I saw."

"What you saw?"

"Yeah, the day before the murder."

I blinked. "I can't give you any money," I said. "That wouldn't be right. But what if I gave you cupcakes or food?"

Shawn licked his lips, glancing down at the tepid soup in front of him.

"What do you say?"

"Yeah, OK. I guess." He ate the last of his bread, slowly. "I think I know who did it for real."

"Who? How?"

Shawn paused for effect. "It was Emmaline."

"What? Who's Emmaline?" My insides had gone icy cold with the certainty that I was about to find out something that would blow my mind, that would, perhaps, change everything. "Shawn?"

"Emmaline is the wife of the guy who lives next door. You know that guy, the one who threw the massive Halloween party?"

It took a minute for the information to click home. "Franklin? Franklin Smith?"

"That's right. So, I think it was his wife 'cause the day before Theresa was murdered, I was hanging out on the roof of my aunt's house, great place to scope out kitchens. People leave their curtains open a lot, and I can see what they're cooking or what they bring home to eat."

I could barely keep track of his words. Emmaline was Franklin's wife. Franklin who had been set on winning the Halloween Day Competition. And Emmaline who had been fired from her job for stealing.

Money. They didn't have money.

"So, basically," Shawn continued, "I was on the roof, right? And I saw Theresa out front. She had this whole amazing setup of Halloween decorations, but the neighbor didn't seem to like that. Emmaline and Theresa got into a fight because she caught the other woman stealing her skeletons. The fake ones. Shoot, I tried to steal them back on the day of the festival, but everyone thought I was just being... yeah, it's whatever."

Decorations. Halloween party. Competition. Cash prize.

The truth struck me between the eyes. I scraped my chair back. "I have to go," I said. "Now."

"Hey, but what about my cookies?"

"Come by the Oceanside later. I'll give you as many cakes and cookies as you want, Shawn." And with that, I sprinted from the soup kitchen, drawing my cellphone from my pocket as I went.

Eighteen

"YOU'RE LYING," JONES SAID, DOWN THE LINE. "I don't believe it for a second. Why wouldn't Shawn have told us that? He's misleading you because he wants money from you." Each sentence was emphasized harshly.

"Look, just get to Franklin Smith's house. Emmaline's the murderer. I'm sure of it."

"This had better not be a false lead. I put you in jail once already. I'd be more than happy to do it again."

I hung up rather than rising to the taunt. Besides, I needed my energy and focus on what was ahead. I rounded the corner and entered the street just off Main, where Franklin's house was located. It was still done up in style for Halloween, basically overflowing with decorations, some of which I didn't doubt had belonged to Theresa.

Or to Sam, for that matter. She'd lost her decorations

overnight. A part of me had assumed that it had been Shawn who had vandalized her guesthouse for the sake of it, but from what he'd told me, it seemed that he had been after food more than anything else.

And that would explain why the person who'd stolen the decorations had trashed Sam's back porch too.

It had to be Emmaline.

I reached the front of the house and stopped, my heart pounding in my throat. Was it so simple? Could it be?

A scream rang out from within. "Help! Help me, please!"

Oh no. Oh no, I can't possibly handle this. But the negative thoughts didn't stop me from rushing toward the front of the Smith residence. The front door was shut but unlocked. I opened it and let myself into a hallway that was devoid of decoration. Odd.

"Please!" It was a woman's voice, coming from the living room.

I entered and stopped on the worn carpet. It was Emmaline. And she was tied to a chair.

"What on earth? What happened to you?"

"It was Franklin," Emmaline burst out. "He killed her! He killed Theresa. I had my suspicions but, I just ... I didn't want to say anything because I was too afraid. Please, help me. He might come back!"

"Don't worry, the police are on their way." Not that Jones was any form of comfort at a time like this.

I untied Emmaline, hurriedly, and she sat down heavily on the sofa, pressing her hands to her eyes. "I can't believe it. I can't believe he actually did it."

"Could you explain?" I had to hear the truth, right from her mouth.

"I always suspected but ... we've been having financial troubles," Emmaline said, "a lot of them. See, um, Franklin has a bit of, a, well, a gambling problem. He spent our life's savings, the money we'd set aside for our retirement cruise, on paying back debts. He said that if we didn't come up with the money soon, we'd lose the house. And then I lost my job, and it was all so dire, and I just ... oh, this is all my fault."

"Can you tell me what happened, Emmaline? Was it because of the Halloween Day Competition?"

Emmaline's flabby cheeks quivered. She rubbed her palms over them, trying to rid them of the tears. "Yes, it was that cursed Halloween competition. Frankie tried to win it every year, but it never worked out. Theresa always beat us to it. She had the mayor in her pocket, but this year, well, Frankie came up with a plan." She swallowed. "He decided he would steal all of Theresa's decorations and trash them, then start collecting as many for himself from the surrounding neighborhood as possible."

"He stole Sam's décor!"

"I did that," Emmaline said, hanging her head. "I was just trying to make it work, but I never, not for a second, thought he would take it this far. He... he... he got into a fight with Theresa on the night of the party. I saw him walk off with her, and I assumed it was because he wanted to make sure she got back to her house OK, but he was missing for quite a while and then—" Emmaline broke into almighty sobs. "He's ruined everything. Everything."

So, Theresa had likely gotten angry and confronted Franklin after finding out that Emmaline had been stealing decorations, and Franklin had snapped. Money did strange things to people.

"Where is he now?" I asked. "Where's Franklin?"

"He said he was leaving, and that I was lucky he'd decided to leave me here instead of killing me. Like our marriage didn't mean anything to him at all."

"Do you know which route he took?" I asked, my fingers itching to hit the dial button.

"No, but he did say he was heading for the Canadian border."

Quick as a flash, I put the call through to Jones. The detective huffed and puffed and grumbled, but the chase was on. I could only trust that he would bring Franklin the murderer down before it was too late.

Nineteen

Three days later

"I'm telling you, I'm fine. I can go back on the... the... choo!" Bee sneezed into her Kleenex and dared me to say anything with a watery-eyed stare.

"That settles it," I said. "No food truck until you're officially free of the sneezes."

"So not fair. I'm not infectious anymore," Bee said. "The doctor said so."

"He said no such thing, and your nose is dribbling again."

"Ugh." Bee wiped and settled back against the extra

cushions on the bed. "This is terrible. I haven't been out of the guesthouse in days. I'm missing all the fun."

"The fun?"

"I didn't get to see Franklin getting arrested."

"True. And it was quite spectacular."

Bee's hazel eyes glazed over. "Tell me about it again. I love a good bedtime story."

"All right, but only because this one isn't spooky." I reached over and checked her pillow was straight, then positioned myself in one of the comfy, floral-patterned armchairs in Bee's room. "It was the night before Halloween, and all through the—"

"C'mon, get to the good stuff."

"So impatient." I giggled. "All right, so it turns out, Jones didn't need to go all the way out of town to catch Franklin. They found him at a gas station near the cove. He'd been going in the wrong direction and had stopped to purchase a map."

"To Canada. A map to Canada." Bee laughed. "These are tears of joy, by the way. They've got nothing to do with the flu. Had the man never heard of GPS? I mean, there are apps on our phones that will take us wherever we need to go."

"Ask me no questions, and I'll tell you no lies."

"Tell me more."

"Like, he did have a car," I replied, bobbling my head and imagining the tune to one of the songs in *Grease*. "And it's now impounded. Franklin wanted the money from the competition, but as it happens, it wasn't to pay off his debt. It was because he wanted to abandon poor Emmaline with all that debt and rush off across the border to start a new life."

"That's a special breed of idiot."

"Indeed. A cruel one. Anyway, Jones chased Franklin halfway across the parking lot before he caught him, and what's really funny is that neither of them is particularly fit, so it was kind of like two fluffy teddy bears chasing each other between the gas pumps. Detective Martin told me."

"That has truly made my entire week. I can't get tired of hearing that story."

A knock sounded at the bedroom door, and Sam poked her head around it. "Hi there," she said. "Sorry to interrupt, but I thought you might like more chicken soup?"

"Again," Bee sighed. "I've had enough chicken soup to last me a lifetime. So much, in fact, that I could produce it at will."

"I definitely don't want to know how," I replied. "Or where it would come from."

Sam placed the tray on the bedside table. "I know it's boring, Bee, but it's good for you. Besides, I put carrots and celery in it this time."

"I'm all a-tingle with excitement."

"Don't mind her, Sam. She's just upset because she's confined to her bed. You're a real Nightingale, and Bee is very grateful. Aren't you Bee?"

"Yes, very grateful," she said, eyeing the soup.

I got up and moved over to the coffee and tea station in the corner of the room. "Can I make you a cup, Sam?"

"That would be great. That new assistant is running me ragged."

"He is?" Butterflies tumbled through my belly. Sam could now afford to hire extra help, thanks to her competition winnings, and she needed that help in the kitchen in particular. It was me who'd suggested she give Shawn a job. Even though he definitely had a criminal record. Turned out, it had been for breaking into restaurants and stealing food. "Is he behaving himself?"

"Oh, he's fantastic," Sam said. "Amazing in the kitchen. A real talent! It's just he keeps coming up with these long lists of ingredients for the fancy dishes he wants to cook up."

"He's not stealing any of it, is he?" Bee asked, saying what we were all thinking.

"Nothing's gone missing yet. I think he knows that I'm not going to be kind if he messes me around. Besides, we've struck an amicable deal. He can work here and get paid for it, even board in one of the smaller guestrooms, but he's not allowed to wear black lipstick and nail polish. Scares the guests."

"And Trouble," I said, as the kitten padded into the room.

The calico bounded onto the bed and settled on Bee's feet, massaging the end of her comforter. They had struck an uneasy friendship whereby she would allow him to lie on her feet, and he would allow her to, well, have his presence.

"I'm glad everything's working out," I said. "I was afraid that the end of this week would be a disaster."

"Me too." Sam accepted a mug of coffee from me. "But, you know, it's actually been great. I won the competition, I've started planning a remodel for the back porch, and I have a brand new chef who cooks better than I ever could."

"Just as long as he doesn't make me eat anything weird," Bee said, stifling a yawn.

I paused, offering Sam a quick wink. "How about some chicken soup?"

"Ruby Holmes, you and your smart mouth." Bee tossed a cushion at me, and I caught it, hugging it to my chest. "You're lucky it's your birthday next week, or I'd have to punish you for your teasing."

"I think she learned it from you," Sam said.

"Don't you start."

We dissolved into laughter that soon turned to chatter, and for the first time all week, I finally relaxed. Carmel Springs was at peace, Bee would recover, and a cool, fall breeze whispered against the sides of the Oceanside, bringing with it the scent of the sea and the promise of more adventure to come.

Join Ruby and Bee in their next adventure, MURDER AND MERINGUE CAKE, *and find out what's next for Carmel Springs.*

Turn the page to read the first chapter.

Murder and Meringue Cake

CHAPTER 1

"HAPPY BIRTHDAY TO YOU! HAPPY BIRTHDAY TO you," Bee sang, swaying from side-to-side in the food truck. The sun had just started setting, casting its oranges and pinks over the Maine sky and the ocean waves. The beach was placid, the benches in front of our truck empty, and the customers lining up to get their last fix of sweet treats.

We were due to close up shop any second, and I anticipated a night of quiet contemplation, Sam's delicious dinner at the guesthouse, and a bubble bath.

But Bee had other plans.

"Happy birthday to you," my friend continued. "Come on. Everybody sing along."

My cheeks grew warm as the last customers of the day

—all lined up in front of the Bite-sized Bakery food truck —cheered and clapped and sang along.

"Bee," I said, "thank you, but this is not necessary."

"Of course it's necessary," she replied. "It's not every day that a woman turns thirty-seven!" Bee grinned and brought out a cupcake on a plate. She had placed a magenta candle in its center and a cherry off to one side on top of creamy white frosting. "I hope you don't mind, folks, but it's time we celebrate Ruby's birthday."

The customers applauded again.

"You don't have to do this." I couldn't help smiling though. I had never liked my birthday. I'd never had a particularly memorable one, and I didn't see any reason to go ahead and celebrate a day when I was another year older.

Not that there was anything wrong with getting old. At least I'd started living my dream.

But this type of thing *was* important to Bee. The customers huddled closer to the truck's window, watching as my friend lit the candle for me to blow out. I took a breath and blew out the merry flame to cheers and shouts.

"Thank you all, so much," I said, smiling. "And thank you, Bee."

"It's just a cupcake, Rubes. I've got a gift for you waiting back at the Oceanside."

"You really shouldn't have."

Bee had made up her mind. She wanted to spoil me for my birthday. And I wouldn't deny her that if it meant so much to her.

We finished up serving the last of the folks waiting for their treats and coffees or hot chocolates. Each of them wished me a happy birthday then hurried off into the evening, the sky purpling like the lavender dusting on a donut.

The wind was still, but it was cold enough that I needed a thick coat to keep me warm outside the truck.

"Are you ready to go?" Bee rubbed her hands together and grinned.

"Yes, I am," I replied. "Why?" I tilted my head to one side. "You're acting strangely."

"I'm not. I'm just excited to celebrate your birthday with you," Bee said, the tip of her nose red. She'd only just recovered from the flu the week before and had a few sniffs to get over still. "And to give you your gift."

"Bee, you know you don't need to go wasting your money on me." I paid her well—she was a fantastic baker —and we had loads of fun working together. I considered her a good friend, but that didn't mean I wanted her spending her money on me.

"You don't like birthdays, do you?" Bee asked, as we shut the side window on the food truck and made our way around to the front of it. We got inside, and I sighed, shutting my door and then clipping my seatbelt into place.

"What gives you that idea?" I asked.

"Oh, maybe it's the fact that you look more sad than happy. And you went pink as a peach when we sang happy birthday to you."

I shrugged. "I'm not used to all that attention. And I've never really celebrated my birthday before."

"You haven't?" Bee was incredulous. "Not even when you were little?"

"Sometimes I'd have cake, but it was never a big deal. My parents had other things to worry about, like finances. Or deciding whether they wanted to stay together or not."

"Eek. Sorry, I didn't know."

"Of course you didn't," I said. "We don't talk about boring stuff like this."

"It's not boring, Ruby." Bee clipped on her seatbelt. "But if you don't want to do anything for your birthday, that's fine. We don't have to." She shifted and brought her phone out of her pocket.

"No. Let's do what you wanted to do. That sounds fun. Different." The last time I'd celebrated a birthday, it had been with my ex-fiancé, Daniel, and that hadn't exactly gone according to plan either. In that he'd never turned up for the celebration.

Instead, he'd disappeared. And the only way I'd discovered he was still OK and alive was through his family. But he didn't want to see me again.

I pressed my thumb to my ring finger and clicked my tongue. It was past time I forgot about him and all that silliness. "Come on," I said, "let's find out what Sam's cooked us for dinner. And then you can give me a birthday gift."

Bee slipped her phone back into her pocket and clapped her hands. "Perfect. I'm pretty nervous, though."

"You, nervous?"

"I know. So unlike me." She gave me her signature gap-toothed smile, tucking a few strands of silver hair behind her ears. "It must be the flu. It weakened not just my immune system but my emotional state. I wonder if they make medicine for that."

I laughed and steered the food truck down the road toward the Oceanside. I parked out front and frowned, peering up at the guesthouse. The lights were off. "That's strange. I thought Sam would be home."

"Maybe she forgot it was your birthday," Bee said. "She might have gone out to the Lobster Shack now that it's reopened."

"Heavens, I wonder if they're finally serving lobster there again."

"From what I heard, Benjamin's finally squashed his beef with the owner of the wharf. And that means lobster rolls," Bee said, licking her lips. "Let's go inside and see if she's there. If not, we can always go catch up with her at the Lobster Shack."

"That sounds good."

We got out of the truck, and Bee charged ahead of me, up the steps of the guesthouse. My frown deepened. It was so terribly quiet, and it sort of gave me the creeps. Halloween had been more than a week ago. The decorations had been taken down, and there hadn't been any other murders or incidents in Carmel Springs since then.

Bee unlocked the front door, and we entered.

"Goodness, it's dark," I said, stumbling in after her. "Usually Sam leaves the hall lights on."

"Here," Bee said and grabbed hold of my arm. She guided me a few steps into the guesthouse. "Almost. Just a few more steps."

"Huh? What are you talking about?"

The lights flicked on. At least twenty smiling faces greeted me followed by a roar of, "Surprise!"

I let out a cry, my hands flying to my face. Shock was quickly replaced by pleasure and excitement. My heart pounded away, and a giggle escaped me.

"Happy birthday," my friends chorused. Bee clapped and hopped up and down on the spot next to me.

"A surprise par—" But I cut off, my gaze shifting to the

long table where the gifts had been gathered. The gifts and something else. *Someone* else.

Another scream broke through the shouts and applause. And then another and another as the people in the room saw exactly what I had seen.

Detective Jones's body, draped across the sparkling wrapped gifts, the end of a silver knife sticking out of his back.

Keep reading by grabbing your copy of MURDER AND MERINGUE CAKE today on any major retailer!

More for you...

Sign up to my mailing list and receive updates on future releases, as well as **FREE** copies of *The Hawaiian Burger Murder* and *The Fully Loaded Burger Murder*.

They are short cozy mystery featuring characters from *the Burger Bar Mystery series.*

Head over to rosiebooks.shop to get your free books!

Craving More Cozy Mystery?

If you had fun with Ruby and Bee, you'll, love getting to know Charlie Mission and her butt-kicking grandmother, Georgina. You can read the first chapter of Charlie's story, *The Case of the Waffling Warrants,* below!

"Come in, Big G, come in." I spoke under my breath so that the flesh-colored microphone seated against my throat picked up my voice. "What is your status?"

My grandmother, Georgina—pet name Gamma, code name Big G—was out on a special operation. Reconnaissance at the newest guesthouse in our town, Gossip. The reason? First, she was an ex-spy, as was I, and second, the woman who'd opened the guesthouse was her mortal enemy and in direct competition with my grandmother's establishment, the Gossip Inn.

Who was this enemy, this bringer of potential financial doom?

A middle-aged woman with a penchant for wearing pashminas and annoying anyone who looked her way.

Jessie Belle-Blue.

It was rumored that even thinking the woman's name summoned a murder of crows.

"I repeat, Big G, what is your status?"

"I'm en route to the nest," my grandmother replied in my earpiece.

I let out a relieved sigh and exited my bedroom, heading downstairs to help with the breakfast service.

In the nine months since I had retired as a spy, life in Gossip had been normal. In the Gossip sense of the term. I'd expected that my job as a server, maid, and assistant would bring the usual level of "cat herding" inherent when working at the inn. Whether that involved tracking down runaway cats, literally, or providing a guest with a moist towelette after a fainting spell—tempers ran high in Gossip.

What was the reason for the craziness? Shoot, it had to be something in the water.

I took the main stairs two at a time and found my friend, the inn's chef, paging through her recipe book in the lime green kitchen. Lauren Harris wore her red hair in a French braid today, apron stretched over her pregnant belly.

"Morning," I said, "how are you today?"

"Madder than a fat cat on a diet." She slapped her recipe book closed and turned to me.

Uh oh. Looks like it's time for more cat herding.

"What's wrong?"

"My supplier is out of flour and sugar. Can you believe that?" Lauren huffed, smoothing her hands over her belly while the clock on the wall ticked away. Breakfast was in two hours and Lauren loved baking cupcakes as part of the meal.

"Do you have enough supplies to make cupcakes for this morning?"

"Yes. But just for today," Lauren replied. "The guests are going to love my new waffle cupcakes, and they'll be sore they can't get anymore after this batch is done. Why, I should go down there and wring Billy's neck for doing this to me. He knows I take an order of sugar and flour every week, and I get it at just above cost too. What's Georgina going to say?"

"Don't stress, Lauren," I said. "We'll figure it out."

"Right." She brightened a little. "I nearly forgot you're the one who "fixes" things around here." Lauren winked at me.

She was the only person in the entire town who knew that my grandmother and I had once been spies for the NSIB—the National Security Investigative Bureau. But the news that I had helped solve several murders had spread through town, and now, anybody and everybody with a problem would call me up asking for help. A lot of them offered me money. And I was selective about who I chose to help.

"I'll check it out for you if you'd like," I said. "The flour issue."

"Nah, that's OK. I'm sure Billy will get more stock this week. I'll lean on him until he squeals."

"Sounds like you've been picking up tips from Georgina."

Lauren giggled then returned to her super-secret recipe book—no one but she was allowed to touch it.

"What's on the menu this morning?" I asked.

Lauren was the boss in the kitchen—she told me what to do, and I followed her instructions precisely. If I did anything else, like trying to read the recipe for instance, the food would end up burned, missing ingredients or worse.

The only place I wasn't a "fixer" was in the Gossip Inn's kitchen.

"Bacon and eggs over easy, biscuits and gravy, waffle cupcakes and... oh, I can't make fresh baked bread, can I?"

"Tell her I'll bring some back with me from the

bakery." Gamma's voice startled me. Goodness, I'd forgotten about the earpiece—she could hear everything happening in the kitchen.

"I'll text Georgina and ask her to bring bread from the bakery."

"You're a lifesaver, Charlotte."

We set to work on the breakfast—it was 7:00 a.m. and we needed everything done within two hours—and fell into our easy rhythm of baking and cooking.

My grandmother entered the kitchen at around 8:30 a.m., dressed in a neat silk blouse and a pair of slacks rather than the black outfit she'd left in for her spy mission. Tall, willowy, and with neatly styled gray hair, Gamma had always reminded me of Helen Mirren playing the Queen.

"Good morning, ladies," she said, in her prim, British accent. "I bring bread and tidings."

"What did you find out?" I asked.

"No evidence of the supposed ghost tours," Gamma said.

We'd started hosting ghost tours at the inn recently, so of course Jessie Belle-Blue wanted to do the same. She was all about under-cutting us, but, thankfully, the Gossip Inn had a legacy and over 1,000 positive reviews on Trip-Advisor.

Breakfast time arrived, and the guests filled the quaint dining area with its glossy tables, creaking wooden floors, and egg yolk yellow walls. Chatter and laughter leaked through the swinging kitchen doors with their porthole windows.

"That's my cue," I said, dusting off my apron, and heading out into the dining room.

I picked up a pot of coffee from the sideboard where we kept the drinks station and started my rounds.

Most of the guests had gathered around a center table in the dining room, and bursts of laughter came from the group, accompanied by the occasional shout.

I elbowed my way past a couple of guests—nobody could accuse me of having great people skills—apologizing along the way until I reached the table. The last time something like this had happened, a murder had followed shortly afterward.

Not this time. No way.

"—the last thing she'd ever hear!" The woman seated at the table, drawing the attention, was vaguely familiar. She wore her dark hair in luscious curls, and tossed it as she spoke, looking down her upturned nose at the people around the table.

"What happened then, Mandy?" Another woman asked, her hands clasped together in front of her stomach.

Mandy? Wait a second, isn't this Mandy Gilmore?

Gamma had mentioned her once before—Mandy was

a massive gossip in town. Why wasn't she staying at her house?

"What happened? Well, she ran off with her tail between her legs, of course. She'll soon learn not to cross me. Heaven knows, I always repay my debts."

"What, like a Lannister from *Game of Thrones*?" That had come from a taller woman with ginger curls.

"Shut up, Opal," Mandy replied. "You have no idea what we're talking about, and even if you did, you wouldn't have the intelligence to comprehend it."

The crowd let out various 'oofs' in response to that. The woman next to me clapped her hand over her mouth.

"You're all talk, Gilmore." Opal lifted a hand and yammered it at the other woman. "You act like you're a threat, but we know the truth around here."

"The truth?" Mandy leaned in, pressing her hands flat onto the tabletop, the crystal vase in the center rattling. "And what's that, Opal, darling? I'd love to hear it."

"That you're a failure. You sold your house, left Gossip with your head in the clouds, told everyone you were going to become a successful businesswoman, and now you're back. Back to scrape together the pieces of the life you have left."

"Witch!" Mandy scraped her chair back.

"All right, all right," I said, setting down the coffee pot

on the table. "That's enough, ladies. Everyone head back to their tables before things get out of hand."

Both Opal and Mandy stared daggers at me.

I flashed them both smiles. "We wouldn't want to ruin breakfast, would we? Lauren's prepared waffle cupcakes."

That distracted them. "Waffle cupcakes?" Opal's brow wrinkled. "How's that going to work?"

"Let's talk about it at your table." I grabbed my coffee pot and walked her away from Mandy. The crowd slowly dispersed, people muttering regret at having missed out on a show. The Gossip Inn was popular for its constant conflict.

If the rumors didn't start here then they weren't worth repeating. That was the mantra, anyway.

I seated Opal at her table, and she pursed her lips at me. "You shouldn't have interrupted. That woman needs a piece of my mind."

"We prefer peace of mind at the inn." I put up another of my best smiles.

Compared to what I'd been through in the past—hiding out from my rogue spy ex-husband and eventually helping put him behind bars when he found me—dealing with the guests was a cakewalk.

"What brings you to Gossip, Opal?" I asked.

"I live here," she replied, waspishly. "I'm staying here while they're fumigating my house. Roaches."

"Ah." I struggled not to grimace. Thankfully, my cell phone buzzed in the front pocket of my apron and distracted me. "Coffee?"

"I don't take caffeine." And she said it like I'd offered her an illegal substance too.

"Call me if you need anything." I hurried off before she could make good on that promise, bringing my phone out of my pocket.

I left the coffee pot on the sideboard, moving into the Gossip Inn's spacious foyer, the chandelier overhead off, but catching light in glimmers. The tables lining the hall were filled with trinkets from the days when the inn had been a museum—an eclectic collection of bits and bobs.

"This is Charlotte Smith," I answered the call—I would never get to use my true last name, Mission, again, but it was safer this way.

"Hello, Charlotte." A soft, rasping voice. "I've been trying to get through to you. I'm desperate."

"Who is this?"

"My name is Tina Rogers, and I need your help."

"My help."

"Yes," she said. "I understand that you have a certain set of skills. That you fix people's problems?"

"I do. But it depends on the problem and the price." I didn't have a set fee for helping people, but if it drew me away from the inn for long, I had to charge. I was technically a consultant now. Sort of like a P.I. without the fedora and coffee-stained shirt.

"My mother will handle your fee," Tina said. "I've asked her to text you about it, but I... I don't have long to talk. They're going to pull me off the phone soon."

"Who?"

"The police," she replied. "I'm calling you from the holding cell at the Gossip Police Station. I've been arrested on false charges, and I need you to help me prove my innocence."

"Miss Rogers, it's probably a better idea to invest in a lawyer." But I was tempted. It had been a long time since I'd felt useful.

"No! I'm not going to a lawyer. I'm going to make these idiots pay for ever having arrested me."

I took a breath. "OK. Before I accept your... case, I'll need to know what happened. You'll need to tell me everything." I glanced through the open doorway that led into the dining room. No one looked unhappy about the lack of service yet.

"I can't tell you everything now. I don't have much time."

"So give me the *CliffsNotes*."

"I was arrested for breaking into and vandalizing Josie Carlson's bakery, The Little Cake Shop. Apparently, they found my glove there—it was specially embroidered, you see—but it's not mine because—" The line went dead.

"Hello? Miss Rogers?" I pulled the cellphone away from my ear and frowned at the screen. "Darn."

My interest was piqued. A mystery case about a break-in that involved the local bakery? Which just so happened to be run by one of my least favorite people in Gossip?

And when I'd just started getting bored with the push and pull of everyday life at the inn?

Count me in.

Want to read more? You can grab **the first book** in *the Gossip Cozy Mystery series* on all major retailers.

Happy reading, friend!

www.ingramcontent.com/pod-product-compliance
Lightning Source LLC
LaVergne TN
LVHW041200131224
799041LV00015BA/269